Before he could activate his lightning-quick reflexes, she went up on her toes and kissed him on the cheek.

Then she turned back to the vending machine. Over her shoulder, she said, "Couldn't help it. You're cute when you get befuddled."

He was willing to concede that she was smarter than he was...and probably a better leader...and, very likely, she was more confident. But he wasn't about to let her take the lead when it came to what happened between them.

He was the bodyguard. He was in charge.

He grasped her upper arm and spun her around to face him. Holding her other arm to anchor her to one spot in the bland, empty break room, he kissed her. Not a belittling peck on the cheek, but a real kiss on the lips. His mouth pressed firmly against hers, he tasted mint and coffee. Though their bodies weren't touching, the heat that radiated between them was hotter than a furnace.

MOUNTAIN SHELTER

USA TODAY Bestselling Author

CASSIE MILES

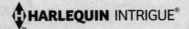

HARLEQUIN INTRIGUE®

Hello, Gorgeous! To my sister, Marya Hunsinger.
And, as always, to Rick.

Recycling programs
for this product may
not exist in your area.

ISBN-13: 978-0-373-69949-0

Mountain Shelter

Copyright © 2016 by Kay Bergstrom

Printed in U.S.A.

Cassie Miles, a *USA TODAY* bestselling author, lives in Colorado. After raising two daughters and cooking tons of macaroni and cheese for her family, Cassie is trying to be more adventurous in her culinary efforts. She's discovered that almost anything tastes better with wine. When she's not plotting Harlequin Intrigue books, Cassie likes to hang out at the Denver Botanical Gardens near her high-rise home.

Books by Cassie Miles

Harlequin Intrigue

Mountain Midwife
Sovereign Sheriff
Baby Battalion
Unforgettable
Midwife Cover
Mommy Midwife
Montana Midwife
Hostage Midwife
Mountain Heiress
Snowed In
Snow Blind
Mountain Retreat
Colorado Wildfire
Mountain Bodyguard
Mountain Shelter

Visit the Author Profile page at Harlequin.com for more titles.

CAST OF CHARACTERS

Jayne Shackleford—A brilliant neurosurgeon who developed a pioneering method for treating stroke victims, she's a little bit clumsy in everyday life.

Dylan Timmons—Not a typical bodyguard, he's one of the owners of TST Security, a computer whiz and a totally sexy self-confessed nerd.

Detective Ray Cisneros—From the Denver Police Department.

Eloise—Jayne's assistant.

Wayne (Woody) Woodward—An FBI special agent.

Peter Shackleford—Jayne's wealthy, powerful father, whose business interests include oil and aviation.

Javier Flores—The handsome Venezuelan businessman shares many interests with Jayne's father.

"Tank" Sherman—This talented hacker has bitten off more than he can chew.

Diego Romero—Longtime leader of a Venezuelan drugs and smuggling cartel.

Martin Viktor Koslov—The assassin would have no problem killing Jayne. Kidnapping her is much more complicated.

Henry and Cordelia Cameron—One of Jayne's patients and his wife.

Tom and Betty Burton—Caretakers at RSQ Ranch.

Sean Timmons—Dylan's brother, a part owner of TST Security.

Mason Steele—The third owner of TST Security.

Chapter One

With eyes wide open, Jayne Shackleford stared at the glowing numbers on her bedside clock: 9:29. Though it didn't really make a sound, she heard *tick-tick-tick*. She rolled over so she couldn't see the number switch to 9:30 p.m., which marked a sleepless half hour in bed.

She wanted a full eight to ten hours of deep, delta-wave slumber before she performed the operation tomorrow morning. Was anxiety keeping her awake? It shouldn't. Her success rate with this neurosurgical procedure was nearly 100 percent: thirty-three operations and only one partial failure. That patient hadn't died, but the surgery didn't erase the effects of his stroke. She had this procedure in the bag. There'd be no problems. Why so tense?

Possibly, she was overly eager, like a kid waiting for Christmas. About an operation? *Tick-tick-tick*. But she couldn't imagine any other pending moment of excitement.

Flinging out her arm, she reached for the wineglass on the bedside table. She didn't take sleeping pills, but she'd found that a glass of merlot before diving between the covers helped her ease into REM.

Her fingers brushed the glass. It slid off the night-stand and fell to the floor. "I'm a klutz!"

The irony annoyed her. She could perform delicate microsurgery without a slip, but when it came to regular life, she was the queen of clumsy, barely able to walk across a room without tripping over her own feet. Her nanny used to say that Jayne was so busy racing to the summit that she couldn't bother to look where she was going. Well, yeah! How else had she gotten to be a top-rated neurosurgeon by the time she was twenty-eight?

Though tempted to ignore the spill, she didn't want to ruin the pale peach Berber carpet that had taken several hours and the advice of two interior designers to select. She sat up on the bed and clapped to turn on the lights. Nothing happened. She clapped again, an un-deserved ovation. No glow.

Pushing her long brown hair away from her face, she reached for the switch on the lamp and flicked it. The light didn't turn on. And the digital clock had gone dark. Her electricity must be out, which meant she'd have to go down into the creepy basement to the fuse box. *Well, damn.* This wasn't supposed to happen. After the last bout of piecemeal repairs on her two-story house, the electrician promised her that she wouldn't have prob-lems. At least, not until the next time she did renovations.

And then, the neighbor's dog sent up a howl.

As if she needed another annoyance?

The chocolate Lab, with dark brown fur almost the same color as her long hair, wasn't usually a barker, but these occasions when he—or was it female?—dashed around woofing reminded her why she didn't have pets. Barefoot, she padded to the window and peeked through the blinds at her usually quiet neighborhood in the Washington Park area of Denver.

Peevishly, she noted that everybody else's lights were on. Looking down from the second floor, she saw the Lab dashing back and forth at the fence bordering her yard.

She should yell something down at it. What was the animal's name? Something with a *k* sound, it might be Killer or Cujo.

The light at the top of her neighbor's back steps went on and potbellied, bald-headed Brian appeared in the doorway. He called to his dog, "Cocoa, hush. Is something wrong? What's wrong, Cocoa?"

Did he expect an answer? Jayne simply couldn't abide people who spoke to their pets. Though she had high regard for the intelligence of nonhumans, she didn't like to see animals treated in an anthropomorphic manner, i.e., asking their opinion or dressing them in doll clothing. Such interactions lacked focus and functionality. In this case, however, Brian's voice had an effect. Cocoa ceased to woof, charged toward the house, crashed up the back stairs and through the door.

The neighborhood was tranquil again. Jayne looked down at the five-foot-tall chain-link fence covered with

English ivy that was already starting to turn crimson in late September. As far as she could tell, there was nothing to bark at.

She opened the blinds so she could use the moonlight glow through the window to see. Going down to the basement meant she needed something on her feet. As she slipped into her moccasins, she heard noises from downstairs. Not the *tick-tick-tick* of a soundless clock, but a click and a clack and the squeak of a floorboard. The sound of a door being opened. Footsteps.

Impossible! No way could an intruder break in. She'd purchased a state-of-the-art security system that set off an alarm and called the police if a door or window was compromised. The system worked on battery even in a power outage. Jayne had specifically asked about the backup—electricity was fragile.

She crept around the edge of her bed to the night-stand where her cell phone was charging. She wanted to be able to call 911 if she heard anything else. Her thumb poked the screen to turn it on. There was no response, no perky logo, not even a welcoming beep. What was wrong with this thing? There had to be enough juice— it had been charging for the past hour. She held the phone close to her nose and pressed in various spots. The screen remained blank.

The noises from downstairs became more distinct. She was almost certain that she heard heavy footfalls crossing the bare wood kitchen floor. The amygdala in the frontal cortex of her brain sent out panic signals, causing her pulse to accelerate and her muscles to tense. If she had an intruder, what should she do? Fight or flight? Fight wasn't her forte. She didn't own a gun and knew nothing about self-defense. Maybe she could hide…under the bed…or in the closet.

Any hope that she might be imagining this nightmare vanished when the third step from the bottom of the staircase squawked. The flicker of a flashlight beam slid across the carpet onto the landing outside her bedroom. *Flight, baby, flight.*

There was only one place to run. She dove into the small adjoining bathroom and closed the door. Not exactly a fortress. The door was flimsy; the lock wouldn't hold. She had to find something to brace against the door.

The beam from the intruder's flashlight shone under the lip of the bathroom door. He was right outside, only a few feet away from her. The knob rattled as he turned it.

She tore down the stainless-steel rod that had been holding the shower curtain around the old claw-foot bathtub. Thank God, she hadn't remodeled in here yet. Thrashing and yanking, she managed to brace the pole between a cabinet and the door.

"Jayne," he whispered, "let me in. I won't hurt you."

Damn right, you won't. "I called nine-one-one."

"I don't think you did." He kept his voice low, but she detected a hint of an accent. "I don't think your phone works."

He must have done something to disrupt her cell-phone signal. And turn off her security system. And cut her electric.

He was smart.

And that was bad news for her. He'd be able to figure a way around her crude door brace in seconds. She couldn't just stand there, wringing her hands. She needed to escape.

The narrow window was her only outlet. If she could get the old paint unstuck and open the glass, she could slide down three or four feet to the slanted roof that covered the wraparound porch. From there, she could lower herself past the eaves to the porch railing.

He pounded the door. "Open up, Jayne."

Using her hairbrush as a wedge, she forced the sticky window latch to release. Frantically, she shoved the glass open. A brisk autumn breeze whooshed inside, and she shivered. Her skimpy cotton nightie wasn't going to provide much warmth. There were beach towels on the top shelf of the cabinet near the door. One of those would have to do.

She grabbed a towel, threw it around her shoulders like a shawl and leaned closer to the door to listen. It seemed quiet. Had he left? She put her ear to the door. Her panic spiked.

What was worse than an intruder who had you trapped in the bathroom? *Two intruders*.

She heard them whispering. They were plotting together, and it wouldn't take them long to determine that she was going out a window. She had to move fast.

She threw the oversize towel with an orange-and-yellow sun out the window, and then she followed, slipping through the bathroom window and down the bricks to the slanted roof over the front porch. The angle wasn't steep, but her footing felt precarious. As she wrapped the sunny-colored towel around her shoulders, she realized that she'd brought the hairbrush with her. A weapon?

The bedroom window to her right lifted. The head and shoulders of a man wearing a black ski mask emerged. He was coming for her. The synapses in her brain fired like a pinball machine. She screamed.

His buddy might already be downstairs on the porch, waiting for her to drop into his lap. She glanced up at the narrow bathroom window. No way could she climb back in there.

He spoke in his whispery voice through the mask, "Be careful, Doctor. I don't want you to get hurt."

"How do you know I'm a doctor?"

"I'd be happy to explain."

He held out his arm, beckoning her toward him. In the moonlight, she saw what he held in his hand. "You've got a stun gun."

He didn't bother with a denial. "I don't want to use it."

He sure did. His plan was to zap her into a state of helplessness and carry her away. Anger cut through her fear. Using all her strength, she pulled back her arm and fired her hairbrush at him.

She was surprised that she actually hit him. And so was he. The intruder dropped his stun gun.

In the moonlight, she could barely see the outline of his weapon against the dark gray shingles. She scampered forward, grabbed the gun and brandished it. "Don't come near me."

He swung his leg over the windowsill.

She went to the edge of the roof. Climbing over the gutter attached to the eaves looked more difficult than she had anticipated. "Help, somebody help me!"

Brian had been on his back porch only a moment ago. She continued to yell. Where was the barking dog when you needed him? "Please help me!"

Her shouts had an effect on the intruder. Instead of climbing out the window, he pulled back inside. Taking advantage of his retreat, she crept across the roof until she was right above Brian's porch, screeching like an emergency-alert siren.

His front door opened. Dumbfounded, Brian squinted up at her. In his left hand, he held his cell phone. From inside his house, Cocoa was barking.

"Nine-one-one," she yelled.

"Your house is dark," he yelled back.

"I have an intruder."

"A burglar?"

Now was not the time for a discussion. "Call the police. Please, please, call."

He gave her the thumbs-up signal and made the call while she perched above the eaves with her knees pulled up. Her long hair fell forward and curtained her face. Though she could have climbed back into one of the windows without too much difficulty, Jayne didn't trust herself to move another inch, not even to grab the towel she'd dropped. Her throat tightened as she gasped for breath. Adrenaline flooded her system.

In her subconscious mind, she must have known something was coming. *Tick-tick-tick*. But she never expected this. Shivering and sweating at the same time, she held her left hand in front of her eyes. Her fingers trembled. A sob exploded through her pinched lips.

Suffice it to say, she would not be getting a restful sleep tonight.

AN HOUR AND ten minutes later, Jayne was still scared. Her hands had stopped trembling enough to type, but her nerves were still strung tight. Wrapped in Brian's green velour bathrobe that smelled like pizza, she sat at the desk in his home office with Cocoa at her side. His house was smaller than hers, only one story, but he worked from home three days a week. The intruders should have come here. Brian's computer equipment was worth more than anything she had at her house.

From the front room and kitchen, she could hear people coming and going, voices rising and falling. It was time for her to rejoin them, but she wasn't ready. All she really wanted was to hide until the danger had passed.

She'd behaved badly when the police officers first arrived to rescue her from the roof. She and Cocoa had both been problematic. The chocolate Lab had been barking and baring his teeth, which seemed like threatening behavior but was, more likely, an adrenal fear response. The dog was scared of all these strangers. Jayne's issues weren't that different.

Frightened, she hadn't known who to trust and didn't like taking orders from anybody. Not the police. Not the paramedic who wanted her to get into an ambulance. She was disoriented. Her neat-and-tidy world had gone spinning madly out of control, and she was so damn scared that she could hardly move.

In Brian's kitchen, a uniformed officer had pulled out a small spiral notebook and started asking questions. Jayne snapped. "Why should I give you a statement? I'll just have to repeat myself when the detective in charge of the investigation arrives."

"Calm down." The officer—a thickset woman with short blond hair—gestured to a chair at the kitchen table. "Have a seat, Ms. Shackleford. May I call you Jayne?"

"It's Dr. Shackleford," she said through tight lips.

"Any relation to Peter Shackleford?"

"My father."

The officer literally took a step backward. When hearing the name, a lot of people kowtowed. Although her father hadn't lived in Denver for ten years, he'd left an impressive legacy including a twenty-seven-story office building downtown and a small airport, both named after the man the newspapers called "Peter the Great."

Jayne hated using her parentage for leverage. She'd left home when she was really young to attend college and hadn't moved back to Colorado until her father was settled in Dallas. Trying not to sound like a brat, she confronted the policewoman.

"Here's what I'd like to do," Jayne had said. "I'd like to take some time alone to calm my nerves and to use my neighbor's computer to type up every detail I remember."

"That's not usually how we do things."

"I have a rational basis for my suggestion." She had explained that much of her work in neurosurgery focused on memory. According to some theories, it was best to write things down while adrenaline levels were high. She had colleagues who would disagree, and her words were taking on the tone of a lecture. "Without the sharp focus engendered by panic, the brain may sort details and bury those that are too terrifying to recall."

The policewoman had patted Jayne's shoulder. "Tell you what, Doc. You can take all the time you need."

Hiding out in Brian's office had given her a chance to catch her breath. She'd finished her statement for the police, printed it and sent a copy to her email. She should have emerged, but fear held her back. The tech-savvy intruders had chosen her house for a reason. She had no idea why, but she felt the pressure of danger coiling around her.

Cocoa rested his chin on her thigh and looked up at her. He truly was a handsome animal. She gazed into his gentle, empathetic brown eyes. He'd tried to warn her.

"I misjudged you," she murmured as she stroked the silky fur on the top of his head. "I thought you were a pest with all that running around and barking."

Not a good sign…she was talking to the dog.

There was a tap on the office door, and Cocoa thumped his tail twice—a signal that the person at the door was friendly, probably Brian. If a police officer had knocked, Cocoa would have growled.

Swiveling to face the door, she said, "Come in."

In a quick move, a man with glasses and a ponytail stepped inside and closed the door behind him. He confronted her directly and said, "I'm the guy."

Chapter Two

Jayne would have reacted to "the guy" with more hostility, but she'd used up her quota of snarkiness for the day. Besides, Cocoa seemed to trust this person. With much tail wagging, the chocolate Lab bounced toward the stranger, who reached down to scratch behind the dog's ears.

She cleared her throat and pushed her messy hair off her face. "What guy?"

"The one who can repair your security system."

She vaguely recalled a two-minute conversation with Brian. When she told him that her home alarm system had been compromised and her cell phone wouldn't turn on, Brian might have said something like *I know a guy who can fix that*. And she might have said that she wanted an appointment with that guy.

"I didn't expect you tonight," she said.

"Fine with me. I like being unexpected."

"How so?"

"Since I'm buds with Brian who's an IT specialist and I know how to repair your system, you might think

I'm all about computers. You'd be surprised to learn that I'm also the part owner of a security firm with a license to carry a concealed Glock 17."

To prove his claim, he pivoted and flipped up the tail of his plaid flannel shirt to show a holster attached to his belt. He turned to face her, pushed his horn-rimmed glasses up on his nose, grinned and said, "Ta-da!"

In spite of her fear, she had to grin back at him. "Did they send you in here to bring me out?"

He shrugged. "I don't have much luck at rock-paper-scissors."

Her initial impression was *NERD* in capital letters. He certainly wore the uniform: glasses, baggy plaid flannel, jeans rolled up at the cuff and a purple base-ball cap on backward.

Then she took a second look—a lingering assessment from head to toe. She tilted her head, and her hair rippled all the way down her back. Though she was seated and not able to judge his height accurately, she estimated that he was well over six feet tall. The wide shoulders under that flannel shirt were impressive but he wasn't bulky. His body was long and lean. His wrists were muscular, and he wore an expensive dive watch. Behind those dorky horn-rims, his eyes were a smol-dering shade of gray.

Unexpectedly, very unexpectedly, she was attracted to him. *Tickity-tick-tick-tick.* Maybe he was her early Christmas present. "Do you have a name?"

"Dylan Timmons." He held his hand toward her and then curled the fingers inward for a fist bump.

She tapped her knuckles against his. "Jayne Shackle-ford."

"I thought you might prefer a bump. Being a neuro-surgeon, you have to take good care of those hands."

"I'm not that much of a prima donna." She frowned, thinking of the way she'd behaved with the police. "At least, I try not to be."

He placed her cell phone in her hand. "They said I could give this to you."

The screen flashed on, and she felt a glimmer of hope. "You fixed it."

"The phone fixed itself. Somebody used a signal-jamming device to disrupt your signal."

"That's just wrong," she said.

"But not illegal. I've heard that pastors are using jammers during their sermons."

Now that she had the cell phone, her mind jumped to practical concerns. "I might need to cancel my sur-gery for tomorrow morning. I should get a good night's sleep before I operate."

"Why so much?"

"The surgery takes five or six hours. I'm not in-tensely involved the whole time, but I need to be alert."

Still, she hated to cancel. Rescheduling the staff was a hassle. A guest neurosurgeon from Barcelona would be observing. Jayne had prepared and reviewed the most recent tests, neuroimaging, PET scans and MRIs. Starting over at another time was an inconvenience for the medical personnel involved. But postponement was much worse for the patient, who had already checked into the hospital, and for his family and friends.

He asked, "What kind of surgery is it?"

"It's not life threatening. Using implanted electrodes, I hope to stimulate the brain so the patient can regain the memory functions he lost after a stroke. The patient is actually awake through much of the procedure."

"Cool."

And she should be able to handle it. "I'll wait until tomorrow to make the decision whether to postpone or not."

"But you need more sleep," he said. "I can start repairs on your alarm system tonight if you're ready to go back into your house."

"No," she said quickly. "Not ready. Not tonight."

After she'd seen the police charge through the front door with guns drawn to search for intruders, she'd never again be able to think of her home as a sanctuary. She felt attacked, violated. Might as well close it up, burn it, sell it. Jayne was ready to call the real estate agent and hand over the keys.

Dylan brought her back to reality. "Where do you plan to sleep?"

With you. The words were on the tip of her tongue, but she kept from saying them out loud. She'd done enough inappropriate blurting for one evening. "I don't know."

"Is there anybody you can call?"

Her cell-phone directory was filled with colleagues and acquaintances from all around the world, ranging from the president of the American Association of Neurological Surgeons to the teenager who shoveled her sidewalks in winter. But there was no one she could call to come over and take care of her. No one she could stay with at a moment's notice.

She pushed the hair off her face and looked up at the surprisingly handsome man who stood before her. "You said you owned a security firm. Do you ever work as a bodyguard?"

"I do, TST Security."

She rose from the swivel chair and straightened the sash on the Brian's dark green bathrobe. "I'd like to hire you."

"You're on," Dylan said without the slightest hesitation. It was almost as though he'd been waiting for her to ask.

"I've never had a bodyguard before."

"Then I'm the one with experience. I've got only one rule—don't go anywhere without me. For tonight, I'll put together your suitcase and book a hotel room. Do you have a preference?"

She was so delighted to have somebody else taking care of the details that she wouldn't dream of complaining. "Anything is fine with me."

"Write down the clothes, including shoes and toiletries, that you want me to pack for you."

Her excitement dimmed when she thought of him

pawing through her things, but the alternative—going back to the house and doing it herself—was too awful to contemplate. "I'll make that list right now. And there's one more thing."

"Name it."

She held out a flat palm. "Whatever you use to fasten your ponytail, I want it. My messy hair is driving me crazy."

He whipped off his baseball cap, untwined the covered-elastic band and dropped it in her hand. "For the record, I like your hair hanging long and free and shiny."

His fingers stroked through his own mane, and she realized that his hair was lighter than she'd thought. Thick, full and naturally sun-bleached, the loose strands curled around his face and down to his shoulders. Jayne wasn't usually a fan of men with long hair, but "the guy" pulled it off. She couldn't imagine him any other way.

DYLAN HADN'T COME here looking for work. His intention had been a simple response to Brian's call, helping out a friend with a crazy lady for a neighbor. But he was happy with the way things had turned out; spending time with this particular lady promised to be a challenge and a pleasure.

With that extra-large bathrobe swaddled around her, he couldn't tell much about Jayne's body. But he liked the bits he saw: her slender throat, her delicate hands and her neat ankles. Drooling over her ankles probably qualified him for the Pervert Hall of Fame, so he transferred his gaze to her long, thick, rich brown hair. A few strands escaped the ponytail and fell gracefully across her cheek. Never before had the word "tendril" seemed appropriate.

He didn't even pretend to look away. It was his duty to watch her body. He murmured, "I love my job."

"Excuse me?"

"I'll enjoy getting to know you."

Her full lips curled in a wise smile as she accepted the compliment. He'd always believed that smart women were sexier, maybe because of their intensity or creativity or strength.

Then she licked her lips.

He swallowed hard.

"Also," he said, "your break-in is the tip of the iceberg for a very cool puzzle. Your security alarm system is one of the best on the market. Disarming it took technical finesse that's above the talents of the average burglar. Not that I think the intent of your intruders was robbery. After they entered the house, they went directly to your bedroom."

"How do you know that?"

"While you were writing out the list of things you need, I read your account." He gestured to the two single-spaced sheets of paper that lay behind her on the desk.

"How could you read it? The paper is upside-down to you."

"It's a skill." He shrugged. "Do you think they wanted to rob you? Do you have some hidden treasure in your house?"

"I don't keep anything of value at the house."

Why did they break in? Since there were two of them, it didn't seem likely that they were stalkers or that the break-in was for sex. Not his problem. As a bodyguard, he wasn't expected to solve the crime. "Are you ready to talk to the police?"

She held her hand level in front of her eyes. "There's only a slight residual tremor."

"Not enough to register on the Richter scale. Let's move."

Keeping a hold on Cocoa's collar, Dylan guided her from Brian's home office to the kitchen, where a plain-clothes cop sat at the table with Brian. Dylan handed over the dog to his owner and introduced Detective Ray Cisneros, a weary-looking man with heavy-lidded eyes and a neat mustache.

After Jayne shook his hand and gave him her typed statement, she approached the uniformed lady cop. Her name, as it said on her brass nameplate, was E. Smith. Dylan had met her when he first came in.

"I need to apologize," Jayne said. "I'm sorry for the way I behaved earlier. I was rude."

E. Smith darted a suspicious glance to the left and the right as though looking for somebody or something to jump out at her and yell boo. "Um, that's okay."

"Thanks for accepting my apology." As Jayne turned

away from the cop, her moccasins tangled in the over-
long hem of the robe and she stumbled. Quickly recovering, she went toward Brian. "I want to thank you for
being a great neighbor. If there's ever anything I can
do for you, just ask."

Dylan didn't know what she'd done to make everybody mad, but he respected her for facing up to her
mistakes. And she wasn't just offering phony pleas for
forgiveness. Her pretty blue eyes shone with sincerity.

When she returned to the kitchen table with a glass
of water, DPD Detective Cisneros looked up from the
typed statement and smoothed the edges of his mustache. "You work at Roosevelt Hospital, correct?"

"Yes."

"And you're a neurosurgeon. A resident?"

"I completed my residency last year."

"Is that so?"

Dylan heard the disbelieving tone in the detective's
voice and didn't blame him for being skeptical. She
looked too young for such an important occupation. In
the droopy bathrobe with her hair in a ponytail, she'd
have a hard time passing for eighteen.

"It is, in fact, so." She took a deep breath and recited her accomplishments by rote. "I completed college at age sixteen, med school at nineteen, internship
at twenty and fulfilled the requirements of an eight-year
residence in neurosurgery last year. Twice, I've won the
Top Gun Award from the YNC, Young Neurosurgeons
Committee."

If his theory that smart women were sexier was correct, Dylan had hit the jackpot with Jayne. She was a genuine, kick-ass genius.

Cisneros took a minirecorder from the inner pocket of his brown leather jacket, verified with Jayne that it was okay to record her and launched into the standard questions.

"Do you have any enemies? Anyone who would wish you harm?"

"There's professional jealousy. Some of my colleagues wouldn't mind if I vanished off the face of the earth, but none of them are likely to hire thugs with stun guns and stage a break-in. Likewise with patients and the families of patients."

"What about in your personal life? Do you have a boyfriend?"

"Not at the moment," she said.

Dylan stifled a cheer.

"Any bad breakups?" Cisneros asked. "Is there anyone who won't take no for an answer? Or women who think you stole their boyfriends?"

"My personal life is super dull."

"In your statement," he said, referring to her typewritten account, "you quote the intruder as saying he doesn't want to hurt you. Did you believe him?"

"He had a stun gun," she pointed out.

"But he didn't use it."

Cisneros asked half-a-dozen more questions that circled the main issue, trying to get a handle on why the intruders had staged this break-in. They had to be after something.

Jayne's responses weren't real helpful. Not that she was being difficult. She just didn't know why men wearing ski masks had attacked her.

Cisneros glanced down at the account she'd written with such care. Very deliberately, he set those pages aside. His unspoken message was clear. "Maybe they don't want to hurt you, Jayne."

"No?"

"Tell me about your father."

"Please don't call him," she said quickly. "He doesn't need to know about this."

Dylan heard fear in her voice.

Cisneros picked up on it, too. "Are you afraid to tell him?"

"It's not that." Frown lines bracketed her mouth. "It's just... I haven't spoken to him on the phone for a couple of months, haven't seen him since the Christmas before last."

"Is he local?"

"Dallas, he lives in Dallas."

Dylan watched as the cool, sexy, smart woman transformed into a little girl with messy hair. She gazed down at her hands, pretending great interest as her slender fingers twisted into a knot on her lap. Her feet in their scuffed moccasins turned pigeon-toed.

Her father, Peter Shackleford, was rich enough to have an airport named after him. His fortune was tied to the oil-and-mining business, and he had a rep for being smart. Not as smart as his neurosurgeon daughter but savvy enough to surf the waves of business and avoid a wipeout.

Cisneros smoothed his mustache and said, "Could this have been a kidnapping attempt."

"I just told you that I'm not close to my dad." Without looking up, Jayne shook her head. "I can't imagine he'd pay a ransom for my release."

"Does your father have any enemies?"

"Yes."

"Any enemies who might want to hurt you."

She lifted her chin and looked directly at Dylan. "My father isn't a bad man."

He didn't believe her.

Chapter Three

Dylan excused himself to go next door and pack a suitcase for Jayne. He didn't want to listen to her heavily edited version of what a great guy her dad was, and he expected that was all Cisneros would hear from her. Though Dylan gave her points for loyalty to Peter Shackleford, he doubted that she'd score high in the honesty department. He could almost see her digging in her heels. No way would she speak ill of her father even though her mysterious intruders were very likely tied to dear old daddy.

That was Jayne's business. Not his. He was her bodyguard, not her therapist.

Before he left Brian's kitchen, Detective Cisneros ordered Officer E. Smith to accompany him to the crime scene. Cocoa escorted them to the back door and wagged goodbye. The dog needed to stay inside while the strangers on the DPD forensic team ferreted out clues at Jayne's house.

Dylan glanced down at the lady cop, whose short legs had to rush in double time to match his long-legged stride. "Does the *E* stand for Emily?" Dylan guessed. "Or is it Eva, Ellen or Eliza?"

"Eudora," she said. "That's why I go by Smith."

"Nice meeting you, Smith."

"Same here." She had a broad smile and big, strong teeth. Her orange-blond hair stood out from her head in spikes. "Did Jayne give you a list of things she needs?"

"In detail," he said as he took the list from his jeans pocket. "I'm not sure how accurate it is. She's still shaky. Her map of the upstairs of her house shows three separate bathrooms."

"That's true," Smith said. "The weird floor plan is because of the renovations she's been doing on the house since she moved in four years ago. Brian told me all about it."

Dylan had also heard a lot about Jayne and her intense renovating. Since Brian spent a lot of time working from home, his neighbors were a source of amusement. He'd told Dylan how she'd dive in and work like mad on some project, then she'd come to a complete halt while concentrating on her career. For several months, the eaves and porch in the front of her house were painted charcoal gray while the back was sky blue.

Though the electricity at her house had been reconnected, Smith pointed the beam of her Maglite at the back door. "If you look close you can see a couple of scratches from where they picked the lock and the high-security dead bolt."

Since the intruders had already turned off the alarm

system, breaking out a window would have been a simpler way to gain access. The neatly picked locks showed a level of finesse that made him think these guys were professionals. In her written account, Jayne had described a whispery voice with a slight accent.

As he strolled through Jayne's house with Smith nodding to the forensic team, he noticed an eclectic sense of decorating that seemed to mimic the pattern of off-and-on renovations. He believed you could tell a lot about a person from their living space. If that was true, Jayne had multiple personalities.

Her renovated kitchen was ultramodern, sleek and uncluttered. Directional lighting shimmered on polished granite countertops, stainless-steel appliances and a parquet floor. This room told him that a modern, classy woman lived here...not necessarily someone who cooked but someone who appreciated gourmet food.

Walking through the archway into the dining room and living room was like entering a different house. The chairs and tables lacked any sort of cohesive style. The walls were bland beige and empty, without artwork or photographs. The only notable feature was a dusted and polished baby grand piano. From these rooms, he might conclude that Jayne didn't do much entertaining at home and was passionate about her piano playing. The sheet music on the stand was for Scott Joplin's "Maple Leaf Rag."

He caught a quick glimpse of the library opposite the staircase at the front door. The big, heavy, rosewood desk and wall-to-wall bookshelves showed an old-fashioned sensibility and a reverence for tradition. Not like the kitchen at all.

Climbing the carved oak staircase, he noticed the loud creak on the third step that had alerted Jayne to the intruders. The stairs and banister had been cleaned and refinished but otherwise remained unchanged from when the house was built in the 1920s. The same held true for the carved crown molding on the upstairs landing. Again, he had the feeling that she appreciated the work of a long-ago craftsman and was perhaps old-fashioned.

Her bedroom, which had been redesigned in shades of peach and gray, looked like the sanctuary of a fairy-tale princess…a tasteful princess but super feminine with a dainty little crystal chandelier. Set aside on a chair were three stuffed animals, all cats with white fur. The kitties were worn but sparkling clean. Though he didn't see any fresh flowers, the room smelled of roses and cinnamon.

He doubted that anybody had sex in this room. There was zero hint of testosterone apart from the forensic guy who was crawling around on the carpet, peering and poking into the fibers.

Dylan noticed the wineglass on the bedside table. In her account, Jayne mentioned spilling the wine but never said that she'd picked up the glass.

"Excuse me," he said.

The CSI popped up. "Who are you?"

Smith said, "He's with me. Are you about done in here? We need to get some clothes for the owner."

"I'm wrapping it up." Like Smith, he held a Maglite with a beam that flashed wildly when he gestured. "How come we're making such a big deal about this break-in? Nobody got killed."

"A weird situation," Smith said, "what with cutting the power and disabling the alarm system and all. Have you found anything?"

"A bunch of prints, but they all belong to the lady who lives here and her employees—a maid and a cook."

"How did you get them read so fast?" Dylan asked.

"Computer identifications, plus I've got one of those handheld fingerprint-readers." As he stood, he picked his satchel up off the floor. "Everything I need to break open a crime is right in here."

"When you arrived," Dylan said, "was this wine-glass on the floor?"

"No, sir, it was standing right where it is."

"Have you checked it for prints?"

"I'll be doing that right now." He gestured over his shoulder. "I'm done with the closet and the dresser, if you need to pack."

Dylan found Jayne's hard yellow suitcase with spinner wheels in the back of the closet right where she said it would be. The organization of her clothing and shoes was impeccable, and he would have thought she was obsessive-compulsive but those characteristics didn't fit with the casual messiness downstairs. He packed the three outfits that she had described precisely. One was for before the operation, then a pair of baby-blue scrubs and then another outfit for post-op.

When he opened the top drawer of her dresser, there was an outburst of colorful silk and satin. Jayne had mad, wild taste in panties and bras. He held up a black lace thong and a leopard bra. For a long moment, he stood and stared.

She baffled him. A brainy neurosurgeon who wore stripper underwear and played ragtime on her baby grand. Who was this woman? He needed to find out more about her.

The CSI made a harrumphing noise. "I've got two prints on this glass—a thumb and a forefinger. And they don't look like all the others."

"Run them," Smith ordered. "I'll step over here and help Dylan pick out the right undies."

When she rapped his knuckles, he gratefully dropped the thong and said, "I'd appreciate your help."

She lectured on why most women wouldn't want to wear a thong in the operating room and how a sports bra was most comfortable for a long day's work. Her anatomical details were too much information for Dylan.

The CSI had turned away and kept his focus on his handheld fingerprint-matching device while Dylan followed Smith across the landing to the incredible bathroom. With the marble and a fluffy white throw rug, this space was as feminine as the bedroom, but there was a difference. The bedroom was suitable for a princess. The bathroom was meant for a sensual queen.

Smith made quick work of packing the essentials on Jayne's list. They were almost ready to leave when the CSI stepped into the doorway. "I've got a match for these prints."

"And a name?" Dylan asked.

"You're not going to like it."

JAYNE APPROVED OF the downtown Denver hotel where Dylan had arranged for a suite, but she wasn't pleased that he'd called in one of his partners to drive the car to the hotel and accompany them onto the elevator and into the room.

While Dylan stood beside her with one hand clamped around her upper arm, ready to yank her out of there at the first hint of danger, his partner, Mason Steele, drew his gun. Looking like a secret agent from an espionage movie, Mason searched the attractively furnished outer room with the sofa, chairs, table, television and kitchenette. He nodded to Dylan before entering the adjoining bedroom.

Though impressed by their professionalism, Jayne didn't appreciate the show. She had a real life. No time for games. "Tell me again why all this is necessary."

"Standard procedure," he said. "When we take you to a new place, we search. It only seems overprotective because there's nobody lurking in this room. If there was a monster hiding in the closet…"

With a start, she realized that Mason hadn't yet looked in the closet by the entrance. A dart of fear stung her, and she stared at that door, remembering herself in the bathroom when the knob had jiggled. *Don't be scared. It's just a door.* Shivers trickled up and down her spinal column as Dylan helped her out of her heather-blue trench coat. When he opened the door, her jaw clenched.

And nothing happened. The boogeyman didn't jump out. There was nothing to be scared of. The sooner she remembered that, the better.

After he hung up her jacket, he returned to her side. Towering over her, he pushed his glasses up on his nose with a forefinger. "You went through a scary time tonight."

"I'm fine."

"Yeah, you are." Though she refused to meet his gaze, she knew he was watching her and had seen her fear. His voice was low and soothing. "Over the next couple days, you might have flashbacks or be jumpy or tense for no apparent reason. I'm sure you know all about post-traumatic stress. I mean, you're a brain surgeon."

"Not a behaviorist."

"What's that mean?"

"There are many theories about how the brain works, and I can only speak for my own opinion. The source of many emotions can be pinpointed on the naked brain, but it's extremely difficult to control behavior."

"Emotion isn't your thing," he said. "You're into memory."

"With my neurosurgery, I can stimulate old memories that have already formed, but I can't implant new memories without the experience."

"But you don't have to experience something to recall it. I've learned about volcanoes but never seen one erupt."

She hadn't intended to meet his gaze, but she found herself looking into his cool, gray eyes and seeing the sort of deep calm associated with yogis and gurus. At the same time, she realized that her moment of panic and flashback had passed. Dylan had distracted her by luring her into lecturing him about her work.

"Very clever," she said. "You handled me."

He directed her to a side chair upholstered in a patterned blue silk that echoed the colors of the wallpaper, while he sat on the sofa and opened a metal suitcase on the glass-topped coffee table in front of them. After removing a laptop computer, he flicked a switch on a mechanism inside the case. A small red light went on.

"What's that?" she asked.

"It means we can talk freely in here without fear of someone listening in."

The various dials and keyboards in his case were nowhere near as complicated as the equipment she dealt with in neurosurgery. "You can be more technical, Dylan. I'm capable of understanding."

"I don't doubt your smarts," he said. "I just don't expect you to be interested in my security tools."

"Unless I say otherwise, you may talk to me in the same depth you use with your colleagues."

"That won't be too hard." Dylan called out to his partner. "Hey, Mason, do you want to know about the circuitry in my white-noise machine?"

His partner stepped into the bedroom doorway. "As long as it works, I don't care."

She glanced between the two men. Mason was clean-cut and muscular. Dressed in a leather jacket and khakis, he looked like a bodyguard. Dylan was a different story. With his horn-rimmed glasses, his purple Colorado Rockies baseball cap on backward and his long hair, he didn't appear to be a tough guy. And yet, if given a choice, she'd pick Dylan every time. There was something about him that connected with her.

He motioned for Mason to join them as he explained the machine to her. "Much of my equipment is proprietary. I invented this stuff for my own use in security. This machine emits a noise that disrupts any other listening device but is too sensitive for our ears to hear. While we're in this room, we can speak freely."

As a neurosurgeon, she understood the concept of blocking different frequencies of sound, but she didn't understand why this sort of machine was needed. "Who would want to overhear?"

"I have something important to discuss." He glanced toward his partner. "You need to hear this, too."

"Shoot."

"There were prints found in Jayne's bedroom. They were on the wineglass that was on the bedside table."

"I didn't pick up the glass." Revulsion coiled through her as she visualized the man in the ski mask touching her things.

"The fingerprint belonged to Martin Viktor Koslov, a hired assassin from Venezuela who learned his trade with the Columbian drug cartels."

Mason growled, "What kind of trade are you talking about?"

"Think of the worst torture you heard about interrogation methods," Dylan said. "Koslov has worked for Middle Eastern emirs and superrich oil men from his home country. For the past eight years, he's been sighted in the US, including Alaska."

"Why Alaska?" She couldn't imagine why an assassin would take a side trip to Juneau.

"The pipeline," Dylan said. "He's not a bomber or a terrorist, but he's suspected in several murders, thefts and complex arms deals."

Mason looked toward her and asked, "How did you get away from this guy?"

"He said he didn't want to hurt me." She remembered his accent. It didn't sound like Spanish, but she really didn't know. Languages weren't her thing. "Detective Cisneros seems to think he wanted to kidnap me and hold me for ransom so he could get something from my dad."

"Your father is…?"

Dylan filled in the blank. "Peter Shackleford, international oilman with interests in the Middle East and in South America."

Mason nodded. "Kidnapping seems like a neat, logical working theory."

"I'm not so sure," Dylan said. "I'd like more evidence, starting with interviewing the person who disabled Jayne's home alarm system. That hack took a high level of expertise, and I can only think of three or four locals who could pull it off."

"Did you contact them?" Mason asked.

"I'm the bodyguard, not the investigator. I gave their names to Detective Cisneros."

Mason sank back in his chair and rubbed his hand across his forehead. "What do you want me to do?"

"That depends on Jayne." Dylan turned to her. "You had a surgery scheduled for tomorrow morning at eleven o'clock. My advice is for you to postpone."

Though she had been thinking the same thing, she didn't like having her plans dictated by some South American assassin. Koslov didn't rule her life. She took her cell phone from her jeans pocket and checked the time. "It's just after midnight. If I could sleep until nine in the morning, I could operate."

"We don't know what to expect from this kidnapper. He might come after you again. Are you sure you don't want to schedule the operation for another time or have someone else take over for you?"

"I'm the best surgeon for this procedure, possibly the

best in the world." She wasn't bragging, just stating a fact. "Also, I have a relationship with this patient. He's a professor of philosophy in his early sixties. A stroke robbed him of his memory. I can get it back for him, and I don't want to wait."

Dylan regarded her with a measured gaze. "Is his condition life threatening?"

"No, but this is about the quality of his life. He's brilliant and wise. He needs to be able to use his memory."

"Agreed," Dylan said, "but he could wait a few days."

"I want my life to proceed as normal. That's why I hired you as a bodyguard." She rose to her feet as she played her final card. "But if you can't protect me…"

Dylan unfolded himself from the sofa and stood, towering over her. Though she was above average height at five feet nine inches, he was over six feet, maybe six-five. He was taller, broader, stronger. An archetypal male, he was everything a man should be. She felt herself melting.

Gazing down at her, he removed his horn-rimmed glasses and made direct eye contract. "I'll keep you safe, Jayne."

The effect caught her off guard. Desire twitched in her belly. Goose bumps erupted on her arms. She wanted to grab his arm and pull him into the bedroom with her. *No way, absolutely not.* She shouldn't be thinking about sex.

She pivoted, took one step and walked into the chair

beside the sofa. Lurching to an upright position, she marched to the bedroom door, stepped inside and closed it with a loud slam.

Chapter Four

The aroma of fresh coffee twitched in her nostrils. Chords of harp music tickled her ears. *Where am I?* Her usual wake-up alarm was as loud and as harsh as a fire engine, the better to wake her up. Then Jayne remembered that she wasn't sleeping at home.

The harp continued as she lifted her eyelids and saw a man with long, sun-streaked brown hair sitting in the chair beside her bed. Dylan wasn't wearing his glasses...or his baggy flannel shirt...or his baseball cap. His black T-shirt outlined his wide shoulders and lean chest. A handsome man, there was nothing of the nerd about him.

Without thinking, she extended her arm toward him. He caught her hand, raised it to his lips and brushed a kiss across her knuckles before she was aware of what he was doing. The gesture seemed absurd, given that she was wearing flannel pajamas. After being caught on her rooftop in a filmy gown and feeling exposed, she'd chosen the world's unsexiest flannels on purpose.

"Nine o'clock, Jayne."

"I love the harp music."

"It's a wake-up app called *Morning Angels*." He gestured toward two china cups on a silver room service tray. "Coffee?"

"Sure."

Her usual clumsiness was even worse in the morning when she wasn't wide-awake, and she hated to risk slopping a hot beverage all over herself. But it couldn't be helped; she needed caffeine. While she arranged the pillows against the headboard, Dylan went to the windows, where he opened the shades and the filmy drapes. She couldn't tear her gaze away from him. Those jeans were the same ones he'd worn yesterday, still rolled at the cuff. But today they seemed well fitted, not tight but snug enough to outline firm glutes and muscular thighs. Long legs—he had very long legs.

He returned to her bedside and poured steaming coffee from a white room-service pot. He added two dollops of cream and gave it a quick stir before passing her the eggshell-white cup and saucer.

"I never mentioned that I took cream but no sugar."

"If you know your way around the internet, you can find almost anything."

She figured that discovering her coffee preference required a search that went deeper than a quick identification. He'd researched her. On one hand, she didn't like being spied upon. But she was complimented that he'd taken the trouble. Last night, she hadn't been sure he'd want to stick around after she'd slammed the door and thrown out an unveiled threat to fire him.

He took a sip from his cup. "How are you feeling?"

"Are you asking whether I'm alert enough to proceed with the scheduled surgery?"

"I am."

Jayne tasted the delicious coffee and considered for a long moment. "Not sure."

After he fiddled with his wristwatch, the harp music went quiet. "I'm resetting an alarm for eight minutes while you make up your mind. You've already had a bunch of phone calls and—"

"Stop!" She held up her palm to halt him. "About these calls, why didn't I hear the phone ringing?"

"I took your cell phone into the outer room."

"Are you telling me that you came into my room, un-invited, and took my phone without my permission?"

"As your bodyguard, I have to invade your personal boundaries. Coming in and out of your bedroom, even watching you sleep…" He shrugged. "It's part of my job."

"Watching me sleep?"

A warmth that had nothing to do with the hot coffee spread through her body. Though she didn't recall her dreams last night, some of her REM and delta-wave activity had to be about sex. As she lifted her cup to her mouth, she sloshed coffee into the saucer.

"I took your phone," he said, "because you wanted

to sleep until nine, and I was afraid you'd get calls earlier than that."

Reaching for a napkin, she tilted her saucer, almost spilling coffee over the lip. He passed her a napkin which she used to dab at her mouth, then to swab the near spill. "I'm glad you caught those calls. I needed the sleep, and I'm surprised that I got it. After all that happened last night, I didn't think I'd be able to relax."

"Oh, yeah, you relaxed. There was some big-time snoring going on. One time, I peeked in to make sure you weren't being trampled by rhinos."

A lovely image! "Who called?"

He recited from memory. "Eloise, your assistant, needs to know something about scheduling the ER. Mrs. Cameron is worried about her husband's surgery and wants to know if he can eat chocolate-chip cookies later today. Three doctors—Lewis, Napoli and Griggs. And one more."

When he hesitated, she cast a curious glance in his direction. "Are you going to tell me who?"

His eight-minute alarm went off, blasting a noise that sounded like screaming cats in heat. He silenced it. "What's it going to be, Jayne? Are we going to the hospital or not?"

"Why won't you tell me about this person who called?"

"It was your father."

His words hit her with a jolt. She spilled her coffee, with most of the liquid being sopped up by the napkin before she shoved the whole mess onto the tray. "What does he want?"

"He didn't tell me."

Belatedly, she realized that if Dylan was answering her phone, he must be giving some kind of explanation for why she was unavailable. She didn't want wild stories about her intruder to spread all over the hospital. "What have you been telling people?"

"Not a thing. I'm saying that you're not available and you'll call back. Your assistant demanded to know if we were dating, and I told her that she'd have to ask you."

"And my dad? What did you tell him?"

"He was a different story."

She knew he would be. Peter Shackleford, her esteemed-by-everybody-else father, was a man who expected people to take his phone calls, especially his only grown daughter. She figured there would have been loud shouting, threats, demands and a hearty dose of cursing. "What happened?"

"He was at your house."

"Here? My house here in Denver?"

"That's right."

Panic exploded through her. She threw off the covers and charged toward the adjoining bathroom. In the doorway, she pivoted and faced him. "Did you tell my dad where we were staying?"

"Nobody knows we're here. It doesn't do much good to take you to a safe place if I tell everybody where it is."

"And my dad accepted that?"

"He wasn't happy about it," Dylan said. "He called about half an hour ago, and I expect he thinks he can triangulate your phone signal to get your location. But I have my own signal jammer that I attached to your cell phone."

"Another of your proprietary inventions?"

"That's right." He finished his coffee and stood. "We need a plan for the day."

"I'm going to perform the surgery. Give me fifteen minutes to get dressed, and we'll go to the hospital."

"And your father?"

"Later."

She didn't want to deal with him right now, but she had to contact him. He was at the center. If an international assassin/kidnapper had broken into her house because of something her dad had done, he should be the one to fix it.

This wasn't her fault. She'd gotten sucked into this high-stakes game, and she didn't want to play.

LAST NIGHT WHILE Jayne was sleeping, Dylan had done computer searches on her, her father, Martin Viktor Koslov and local hackers who might have helped out Koslov. After a sickening dive into the dark web where you could buy any sleazy thing for the right price, he'd found a set of digital footprints running away from Denver. Well-known cyber-ace, Tank Sherman, was erasing himself, changing to another identity, trying to escape. If Tank had worked with Koslov, the local expert might want to make himself invisible before Koslov erased him.

Martin Viktor Koslov was a ruthless killer whose land of origin was Venezuela. Reputedly, he had garroted, beheaded, shot and stabbed his targets. Never caught, never even arrested, he was known for planning down to the last precise detail. The neatly picked lock on Jayne's back door was typical of Koslov; leaving behind a fingerprint was not.

What had thrown the assassin off his game? Was it the instruction to kidnap rather than kill? Koslov avoided explosives because he'd lost several family members, including his mother, to a bomb explosion. Koslov had a brand of violence that was not inspired by any type of loyalty or ideology; rather, he committed acts of atrocity for the highest bidder. And that might make him an enemy of her father.

Dylan had also found a number of connections between Peter the Great and Koslov. They knew many of the same people, visited the same cities and were both cruel in their own way.

Jayne's dad—the man she defended so fiercely to the DPD detective—wasn't a murderer, but he hired and fired without concern for his employees and didn't hesitate to destroy his competitors. He'd made plenty of enemies. Most were businessmen and women based in the US, but there were a few Middle Eastern sheikhs and South American oil magnates who might consider kidnapping to be nothing more than leverage on the next deal.

When Dylan got the phone call from Mason, telling him that he would arrive at the side entrance in five minutes, he rapped on Jayne's bedroom door. "Time to go."

"Are we coming back here tonight?"

He wouldn't make that decision until later today. Right now there was no time for a discussion. The plan was for them to jump into the vehicle as soon as it pulled up to the curb.

Dylan shoved open her bedroom door. "Now, Jayne."

She was dressed in a pair of dark teal slacks, a matching suit jacket and a shiny black blouse. With her dark hair pulled up in a high bun, her appearance was professional and classic. "Give me a sec, I need to find my sneakers."

He grabbed her sneakers off the floor and lobbed them into the gym bag on the bed where she had packed other clothing items. He zipped the bag and tossed it toward her. "Remember when I said there was only one rule for you when I'm being a bodyguard?"

"Don't go anywhere without you," she recited.

"I lied. There's another rule."

"Which is?"

"When I say go, we have to go."

She stuck her toes into a pair of polished black loafers. "Why are we in such a big rush?"

"No questions. I'm serious." Though he wasn't trying to scare her, Dylan didn't want her to think this was a game. "Your life might depend on your ability to respond to my instructions."

The grin fell from her face as she picked up her gym bag and purse. He grasped her elbow and rushed her through the suite, out the door and into the concrete stairwell. He went first so she'd have to keep up with his pace.

As they descended, he explained, "Lots of abductions occur when the victim is in transit, moving from one location to another. That's why Mason is driving over here to pick us up. It's also why we're taking the stairs. It's too easy to trap you in the elevator."

"I'm glad it's only five floors." Their steps were loud on the concrete stairs, and their voices echoed. "I'm guessing that you aren't carrying my bag so your gun hand will be free."

"Good guess." And he didn't feel guilty about making her drag a heavy burden. All she had was a shoulder purse and her gym bag. He pointed to the bag. "Are your scrubs in there?"

"Lots of stuff—lotion, scrubs, comfortable shoes, a cap that's big enough to cover my hair, extra barrettes and more. These operations take several hours, and it's important to have clothes laundered exactly the way I like them. By the way, you did a good job choosing my undies. The sports bra is just what I need."

"That was Smith's idea. If it had been up to me, I would have picked the red satin bra and the leopard panties."

"Most men do."

Was she flirting with him? He couldn't let himself be distracted right now. Dylan had to keep his focus on getting her to the car without incident.

They rounded the last turn in the stairwell. Both he and Mason were familiar with the layout of this particular hotel. If they had their timing right, Dylan and Jayne would emerge from the stairwell, walk down a short hall and exit onto the street just as Mason pulled up to the curb.

Entering the lobby, he scanned quickly. No heads turned. No one noticed Jayne. He pushed open the exit door.

Bright sunlight hit them smack in the face. Holding her arm, he moved across the wide sidewalk adjacent to downtown's central mall. Mason was waiting in Dylan's dark green SUV.

He opened the rear door, got her seated and followed her inside. The minute he closed the door, Mason drove away. Safe!

"Seat belt," he said to her. "Mason, do you know the door we'll enter at the medical center?"

"Northeast corner."

"That's near my office." She opened her purse and started digging. "I have a key card to use on that entrance."

"It's handled," he said. "We downloaded the hospital floor plan and figured out your routes to and from the OR and your office. Detective Cisneros arranged for key cards and necessary identifications since I'm carrying a concealed weapon and can't go through scanners."

For the first time since he'd met her, Jayne seemed to be impressed. Usually, he didn't care if the clients noticed that TST Security did a solid, professional job, but her opinion was important to him. He liked Jayne and wouldn't mind getting closer to her. After this job was over, he'd like to get close enough to pick out her wild undies.

"What are we going to tell people about you?" she asked. "If I introduce you as my bodyguard, I'll have to explain a thousand times why I need guarding."

The thought had already occurred to him. He didn't consider himself a master of disguise, but he was capable of fading into the woodwork as a computer nerd and—thanks to Mason and his bodybuilding work-outs—Dylan could expand his narrow frame enough to look big and tough. Today, he was wearing a tweed sports coat, jeans and a black T-shirt. His hair was pulled back in a tight ponytail at his nape.

He adjusted his horn-rimmed glasses. "I think I can pass as a professor."

"Interesting thought," she said as she studied his look. "You do have an academic look, but you'd need a whole background story. Somebody would catch on."

"I could be a boyfriend."

Her full lips drew into a circle. "No, no, no, no, no. I don't want to start that rumor. Besides, we don't let friends and family into the OR."

"Much as I'd like pretending to be a neurosurgeon…" He actually would enjoy playing that role. The brain fascinated him. "I don't think your patient would appreciate that disguise."

"Or my insurance carrier."

"I've got it," he said. "I'll be a journalist doing an article on America's hottest neurosurgeons."

"Oh, swell, and doesn't it bother you to reduce the schooling and talent it takes to become a neurosurgeon to an article about physical attractiveness?"

"I'll be a regular old journalist. My catchphrase will be—don't pay any attention to me. I'm here to observe."

"Perfect." Glancing toward the driver's seat, where Mason sat stoically behind the wheel, she lowered her voice. "Do you really think I'm hot?"

"You sizzle, Doc."

At the medical center, a sprawling complex at the edge of Denver's suburbs, he rushed her through the side door and up one flight of stairs. From studying the floor plan, he knew exactly where her second-floor office was located. It spoke well of her status that she had her own small office space with a door that closed. Not much larger than a walk-in closet, the room had one floor-to-ceiling bookshelf, a desk with a chair and two other chairs for guests.

From his web research, Dylan recognized the man who had taken the swivel chair behind her desk.

Jayne stopped short and glared. "Hello, Dad."

Chapter Five

Inhaling through her nose and exhaling through her mouth, Jayne attempted to maintain a calm breathing pattern. Nobody wanted a jumpy brain surgeon; she had a responsibility to her patient to remain calm. The worst thing would be to let her father get her rattled.

Dramatically, Peter the Great rose from the chair and stood behind her desk. His barrel chest puffed out like a rooster. She hadn't seen him in ages, not since she'd bought her house and he came to Denver to tell her it was a dump in spite of the changes she'd made, which she took as a challenge to renovate even more. In his tailored gray pinstripe suit with his neatly barbered chocolate-brown hair, which was the same color as hers, he managed to look decades younger than the age indicated by his birth certificate.

He wore his "concerned" face—an expression that hadn't changed since she'd come home from kindergarten with a bloody nose and Dad had hired a professional boxer to teach her self-defense. There was a crease between her father's dark eyebrows; his chin jutted out and his mouth pulled into a frown.

"Last night," he said in his resonant baritone, "you should have called me to let me know you were all right. I was worried."

It's not always about you. Anger seethed inside her. She wanted to scream and yell and tell him that she could have been hurt, could have been kidnapped *and it was his fault.* But what if it wasn't? What if their suspicions were wrong? She was furious and, at the same time, she felt an ache inside. She wanted to rest her head against his shoulder and cry away her fears and doubts.

Preventing either response—yelling or weeping—Dylan extended his hand and introduced himself as her bodyguard. "I'm the one who kept Jayne from calling you. For her safety, we moved her to a secure location and turned off her cell phone so the intruder couldn't triangulate her signal and find her."

"You're the guy I talked to on the phone this morning, the one who wouldn't tell me where you took my daughter."

"That's correct."

"You've got one hell of a nerve, son."

"Over the phone, I can't accurately verify your identity."

"You sure can. I can send you my photo. Or you can watch in real time while I'm talking on my cell phone."

"The intruder disarmed a high-tech, high-quality alarm system at the house. Hacking a cell phone and transmitting a false identification would be child's play for him."

"Jayne should have used another phone to call me."

"Dr. Shackleford requires several hours of sleep before she performs delicate neurosurgery." Dylan turned to her. "Doctor, you should speak to your assistant, Eloise. I have a few questions for your father regarding Martin Koslov."

He practically shoved her out of the office, and she couldn't have been more grateful. She walked down a short hallway to an attractive waiting room, where two patients sat in comfortable chairs reading old magazines. The medical assistant/receptionist was feeding the gang of tropical fish in the five-foot-long aquarium. With her hair dyed a purplish red, Eloise was nearly as bright as the fish with their streaks of neon blue, yellow and mottled green. She had named her fishy friends and made up fishy stories about their lives.

"Sorry about my dad," Jayne said.

"You don't need to apologize. Meeting Peter the Great is a big deal for me. If I'd known he was going to be here, I would have brought a used plane ticket for him to autograph."

"He's not in the airport business anymore." But he probably flew one of his private planes up here from Dallas. "Maybe he could autograph a used oil can."

"You know, Jayne, I never ever pry, but my fish are totally nosy. Hedda—the black one with yellow stripes—wants to know about your cute male friend with the glasses and ponytail."

"A journalist, he's doing a story on neurosurgery."

Eloise hiked up her eyebrows in an expression of disbelief. "And why was he answering your cell phone at seven-thirty in the morning?"

"We met for breakfast." That was somewhat true. Dylan had insisted that she have a bagel and a couple of bites of bacon from his room-service order.

"Is he going to be hanging around all day?"

"For as long as I am." She went to Eloise's desk and jotted a note. If she moved fast, Jayne might be able to escape without confronting her father again. Though she shouldn't leave the office without Dylan, she felt safe in the hospital. There were guards at the doors; nobody entered without passing through a metal scanner.

"I like older men," Eloise said. "Is your father married?"

"Not at the moment." She slid the note across the desktop. "Would you mind returning these calls for me? Especially to Mrs. Cameron, she needs to be reassured about her husband's surgery. I'm going to slip out so I can review the most recent charts and blood work for Dr. Cameron."

Her dad's voice thundered through the closed door and down the hallway. "How dare that cheesy detective accuse me? I'm a law-abiding citizen."

If Eloise's eyebrows went any higher they would disappear behind a swirl of colorful hair. "Detective?"

"I don't know what they're talking about."

Eloise grasped her arm. "Jayne, what's going on?"

"Don't tell anybody."

"Of course not."

But the story would get out. There was no chance of keeping this juicy secret. It'd go viral. She knew from experience that the hospital was a swarming petri dish of gossip. "Somebody tried to break into my house last night and kidnap me. The DPD detective thinks it might be related to my dad. The guy with the ponytail and glasses is my bodyguard."

One of the other doors leading to the reception room swung open and the short, skinny Dr. Bob, the oncologist, popped his head out. He was a worse gossip than Eloise. "No joke?" He gaped. "You were almost kidnapped? Why?"

Eloise pointed down the hall toward Jayne's office. "Rich father. Peter the Great."

"Wow," Jayne said glumly. "You put it together quicker than the police investigator."

"Doesn't take a rocket scientist," Eloise said. "There's only one reason to be kidnapped—ransom. And your dad's loaded."

The door to her office flung open. Her dad and Dylan spilled into the reception area. Her father did something she never would have expected: he hugged her. His big arms wrapped around her, and she was surrounded by the pine-forest scent of an aftershave that he'd worn since she was a girl.

"I could have lost you," he whispered.

"It wasn't that bad."

"Dylan told me there were two of them, wearing ski masks and carrying stun guns. He said that you had to flee across a rooftop."

All of Dylan's description was true. She hadn't realized how dramatic her escape sounded until her dad said it out loud. She added, "And I took the stun gun away from him."

"My sweet little gal, you shouldn't have to suffer for my mistakes. If it's somebody I know…"

He shook his fist. His pupils were so dilated that his blue iris was reduced to a slender rim. Either he was in an elevated emotional state or he'd been taking advantage of Colorado's legalized marijuana. She assumed the former. Her dad didn't do pot.

He concluded, "You can be damn sure I'll find out who's responsible. And I will make them pay."

Over her father's shoulder, Jayne saw the shocked faces of Eloise and Dr. Bob. Their eyes bulged. Their jaws gaped. The patients waiting in the reception area had dropped their magazines and were watching. She gave her father one last squeeze and stepped away from his embrace.

There was moisture at the corner of her left eye that she refused to believe was a tear. Jayne cleared her throat. "I appreciate anything you can do to help the investigation."

"I'll talk to my friend Razzy." She doubted any of the

other people in the room would be aware that her dad was referring to Rashid bin Calipha, one of the richest men in the world and the leader of a sheikdom. "There have been occasions when your good old Uncle Razzy might have used this Koslov character."

"I'm so sorry to hear that." Uncle Razzy? Oh, please!

"I've got plenty of contacts. I'll check in with my oil people in South America." He pulled his cell phone from his pocket. "I'll start with Javier Flores. He's got an office here in Denver."

"Is he an enemy?" she asked.

"A friend, and he's a good enough friend that he might have information about who wants to hurt me."

Before he could punch in the phone number, Dylan stopped him. "I have to take your daughter away. She needs to prep for surgery."

"Not today," her dad said in a firm, no-nonsense voice. "She needs to take the day off. Somebody else can fill in. One of the other docs can pick up the slack."

"That's not how it works." Her tenderness toward him evaporated like dewdrops under a heat lamp. "This surgery is my specialty. I have a relationship with the patient, and I want him to have the best care."

"Sweetheart, I'm sure you do a great job…"

Was he patronizing her? Her temper simmered.

"…but I need to keep you safe," her dad continued.

What did he intend to do? She'd already hired herself a bodyguard. She'd fled from her house.

Once again, Dylan came to her rescue. He pressed

a cell phone into her dad's hand. "It's a burner, programmed with only one number. We'll use it to keep in touch with you."

"Unacceptable." Her dad thumped his puffed-out chest. "She's coming back home to Dallas with me."

She remembered why she avoided living in the same time zone as her dad. It was just too damned painful. To him, she would always be a sweet little girl who reminded him of her mother, his only true love, who had died when Jayne was seven. He'd gone through half-a-dozen wives since then, but the oil painting that hung over the mantel in every house he owned was her mom, Rachel Shackleford, a well-respected biochemist.

Her dad wasn't being deliberately cruel or belittling. He truly wanted to take care of her. Dragging her back to Dallas was, of course, his first solution to the threat.

But she wasn't a child. After her mom died, she'd grown up quickly. She loved her dad, but she resented his steadfast refusal to accept her as a capable, accomplished adult. He never called her "Doctor" in spite of the years of study and hard work it had taken to gain that title. He never complimented her on her achievements, couldn't be bothered to attend her graduation at the top of her class in med school when she was nineteen.

She stumbled backward a couple of steps and bumped into the fish tank. "Sorry, Dad, I'm not going to Dallas with you. This is my home, my life. And Dylan is right about my needing to prep for surgery."

Before he could respond, she swept through the door into the hallway with her bodyguard following close behind.

RECALLING THE ROUTES from the hospital blueprints, Dylan stayed at her side as she stalked through the corridors in the medical building. They passed offices, a break room and a pharmacy before climbing an open staircase to the second floor. He congratulated himself on remembering to grab her gym bag with the special scrubs and sneakers before leaving her office. In spite of her precise skills and her particular, somewhat fussy, need to have the right clothes, shoes and underwear, Jayne was absentminded. He'd also noticed her tendency toward clumsiness, an endearing trait that made him want to be close so he could catch her when she fell.

Without slowing her pace, she glanced up at him. "Thanks for helping me get away from my dad."

"You're good at handling him."

"Our conversations don't feel good. We're always battling."

"He's a tough guy."

"Yes."

"But he means well." He lightly touched her arm, thinking he'd reassure her. Instead of relaxing, she gasped and pulled away, reacting as though she'd been stabbed by a hypodermic.

He gave her space as they marched along the gray-and-blue vinyl floors. For a bodyguard, a hospital created several problems. The interior was a sanitized labyrinth. There was tension in the air. Most of the staff dressed in scrubs or lab coats that all looked alike, and many of them wore masks. When passing people in the corridor, he scanned their faces. As they walked, he frequently looked over his shoulder to make sure no one was following.

Jayne muttered under her breath. "Why won't he accept that I'm an adult? I bought my own house. I'm renovating. I'm fully capable of taking care of myself."

He nodded. "Uh-huh."

"He has no idea what kind of work I do. I mean, he knows I work with the brain, but he thinks that means curing a headache with two aspirin and a good night's sleep."

"Uh-huh."

"Are you going to stroll along and not say anything?"

"I thought your comments were rhetorical," he said. "Do you want an opinion?"

"Of course I do, as long as you say I'm right and my dad is wrong."

"You're both right." He shrugged. "You're a grown-up and deserve respect. But he doesn't want to treat you like an adult because that means you don't need him anymore. He wants to be needed. Dads are like that."

She came to a complete stop and looked up at him. "That's a really smart explanation. Do you have kids?"

"Not yet."

"I shouldn't have asked, too personal." A pink flush

crept up her throat to her cheeks. "Besides, I already knew you didn't have offspring. And I also know you've never been married."

"Internet search?"

She put her head down and proceeded with long strides into the wide second-story overpass that connected the med center with the hospital. Her blushing baffled him. Why would she be embarrassed about looking him up? That was standard procedure for a first meeting. It seemed to be the marital-status part that bothered her. Was she showing an interest that was more than that of client and bodyguard? He hoped so.

On the hospital side of the overpass, she took an unexpected left turn.

"Wait!" He pointed in the opposite direction. "The OR is that way."

"I need to go to the locker room and change."

Ignoring the double-wide chrome elevator, they descended an enclosed stairwell to the first floor. All the doors along the corridor were clearly marked except for the one nearest a side exit with a key-card lock blinking red for locked. He imagined that door was used by most of the staff when coming and going.

They entered a break room with vending machines, counters, a coffee urn, fridge, microwave and toaster oven. Three women in scrubs sat at three separate tables, reading or texting. An open door on the left led to rows and rows of lockers. There were other rooms beyond. Dylan could hear the sound of a shower.

She stopped in front of a beige locker midway down the third row. The number on top was 374. Jayne twirled the combination lock. Before she could open it, he placed his hand over hers.

"I have a few questions," he said, taking out his cell phone. "I need your full cooperation."

"Shoot."

"Last night, you saw Koslov. Would you recognize him again?"

She thought for a moment. "I'm sure there's a perfect image imprinted somewhere in my brain, but I don't think I'd know him. He was wearing a ski mask. It was dark, and I was scared."

Koslov was careful about hiding his identity. Even after all his research, Dylan had found only one partial photo of a profile. He pulled that image up on his cell phone. "This isn't much, but I want you to take a look. If you see anyone who resembles this man, tell me."

She squinted at his phone screen and shook her head. "Not exactly a clear portrait, is it?"

"It's all I've got."

"I wouldn't know his face, but I'd recognize his voice. He had an accent that I didn't recognize as Spanish but it probably was. I'll listen for him." She removed the combination lock and opened the door.

"How much of the cool equipment do I get to play with?" he asked.

"You aren't sanitized," she said, "so you aren't allowed in the OR. But you're free to observe. The neurologists use computers and electronic equipment that you'll find interesting."

"Will you saw off the top of his head?"

"Only in horror movies. But his brain will be exposed throughout surgery."

He jammed his hand deep into his pocket to keep from doing a fist pump. Watching machines that were hooked up inside somebody's brain was astounding. This was real-life, super circuitry. He'd barely tamped down his excitement about witnessing the cool technology when he realized that Jayne was preparing to change clothes right in front of him.

In a calm tone, she explained the difference between an MRI and electro-monitors that pinpointed brain activity. At the same time, she slipped off her teal jacket and hung it in her locker. Without glancing in his direction, she started to unbutton her shiny black blouse. The outline of her black sports bra emerged.

Dylan dragged his gaze away from the milky, smooth skin above her breasts. She wasn't doing a striptease for him, wasn't trying to be sexy at all. And he wasn't supposed to think of her as anything more than a client.

But he'd been a little bit turned-on by a glimpse of her ankles. Seeing the curve of her breast and her slender waist was enough to send him into overdrive. He made a desperate lurch away from her. "I'll go find… something. Bodyguard stuff."

Knowing that he shouldn't leave her sitting in the locker room alone made the situation even more complicated. He hadn't noticed anyone or anything suspicious on their way here, but that was no assurance that Koslov had given up.

Was this long enough to stay away? He didn't want to interrupt her with her pants off, so he stood at the end of the row and peeked around. Jayne sat on the bench in the middle, dressed in scrubs and tying her sneakers. At the other end of the row was a man in burgundy scrubs with a matching surgical cap and a baby-blue mask obscuring the lower half of his face. He moved toward her.

"Jayne," Dylan alerted her. "Do you know this guy?"

She bounded to her feet and took a good, hard look at the stranger. Then she shook her head and frowned. "Not sure."

When the masked man stuck his hand into the pocket of his scrubs, Dylan stepped in front of Jayne and eased his gun from the holster. "Identify yourself."

The man held up an ID and a gold badge. "Special agent Wayne Woodward, FBI."

Chapter Six

"Take off the surgical mask."

The stranger in scrubs pulled the mask below his chin, thrust out his arm and waggled his FBI badge.

Dylan estimated that the population of the Denver metro area was near three million, which meant that law enforcement personnel numbered in the thousands. As part-owner of TST Security, he'd met dozens of cops, deputies and agents. But there were only a handful he knew well. Special agent Wayne Woodward was one of them.

Reluctantly, he introduced him to Jayne. His relationship with Woody was the opposite of friendly, but they shared an interest in computer technology. Often they found themselves hacking away at the same cybercrime.

Dylan put away his gun. "I'm surprised to see you out of the office."

"I could say the same about you."

"Did Cisneros contact you?"

"Kidnapping," Woodward said. "It's FBI jurisdiction."

"Wait a minute." Jayne held up her palm. "Nobody has been kidnapped. I'm standing right here."

"She's right," Dylan said. "Kidnapping is only a theory. The only real crime that's happened is breaking and entering."

Woody sucked in his cheeks and pursed his lips, thinking. He was a careful man. "My office should have been involved from the start." Dylan was reluctant to give up control. Jayne had a tendency to be irritating, but it was his job to keep her safe. More than that, he wanted to protect her, to swaddle her sharp edges in cushioned layers of safety.

Pointing down the row of lockers toward the exit, he tried to herd her out the door and away from Woody. "Dr. Shackleford is expected in the operating room."

Jayne balked. "Agent Woodward," she said, "you can lose the surgical mask. It looks ridiculous, and you won't be getting close enough to my patient to contaminate anything. Another hint—most surgeons and surgical nurses don't wander around wearing their scrub caps, not unless the cap is extra fabulous. Like mine."

She tucked her long, heavy hair into a pastel-blue surgical cap with a design that resembled tangled branches or spiderwebs. Dylan recognized the pattern. "Neuron art."

"Yes." She gave him a quick nod of approval, and then her gaze turned cool again. "As you know, Dylan, I had hoped to avoid talking about the abduction, but after the scene with my dad, the secret is out. There's no need for you to pretend to be anything more than a bodyguard."

"Got it." He matched her curtness. "I'll try not to appear too smart."

"Not what I meant," she snapped.

"I know." He understood. She had not intended to be insulting. Her standoffish attitude was a shield that she used to hide the real Jayne—the woman who wore sexy panties and was a little bit clumsy.

"I trust that you—" she encompassed both of them in a stern gesture "—gentlemen will be discreet."

They nodded. Dylan noticed that Woodward had yanked off his cap. Not one hair on his head was out of place, no doubt a result of FBI training.

They hiked up the stairwell to the second floor and followed a yellow stripe through swinging doors at the eastern end of the corridor. Over the past couple of years, Roosevelt Hospital had undergone extensive renovation, and Operating Room 1A looked brand-new. The spacious room was sparkling clean with a circle of lights suspended above an adjustable operating table. In addition to the usual IVs and monitors, the neurological tracking and mapping equipment took up two walls.

Dylan stood and gawked like a nerd at his first Comic-Con. There were gazillions of switches, buttons, dials and tubes. One screen was a vertical light table that displayed a series of CT and MRI scans. On another screen, he saw a rotating, three-dimensional image of the brain. He wanted to ask Jayne how all these machines were used, but she was already deep in conversation with another doctor.

Special agent Woodward tugged on his sleeve. "How long before they get started?"

"The surgery was originally supposed to be at eleven."

"I know that," Woody said. "It was posted."

An official schedule meant that anybody who wanted to know where Jayne was would be able to find her easily. Dylan looked toward the corridor, half-expecting to see Koslov. "It's already ten minutes past eleven."

"I'm aware. When do we eat lunch? How long does this operation take?"

"The surgery takes five or six hours," Jayne said. "Once we get started, unauthorized personnel are not allowed in the OR. Dylan, if you'd like to come in right now, change into a pair of scrubs from the supply closet and cover up your shoes with booties."

"Yes, ma'am."

Roosevelt was a teaching hospital, and Jayne's surgery provided an experience worth studying. She was one of the only surgeons in the nation who regularly performed this procedure, and there would probably be students and other docs who wanted to watch.

Dylan pointed to the long, high window and the row of theater-style chairs on a platform looking down at the operating theater. Two young women in street clothes were already there. "That's where you're supposed to sit, Woody."

"Don't call me that." Under his breath, he muttered, "Who the hell does she think she is? Granting me her permission to observe? She doesn't call the shots."

"Yeah, she does. This is her surgery, and she's the boss."

"If I wanted to, I could pull the plug right now."

"Let the doctor do her job." He positioned himself near a nurses station, where he had a clear view of both directions in the corridor. "As long as you're here, we should talk."

"Why would I talk to you?"

"Because I know things."

"Such as?"

He sounded like he was offended, as if the FBI deserved more consideration. Dylan knew other agents who cared deeply and passionately about their work. Woody wasn't so inspired. He worried about not having enough time for lunch. A nine-to-five kind of guy, he was a nitpicker...not that there was anything wrong with knowing the details. He'd probably done his homework on this case. If Dylan played his cards right, he might tease some useful information from Woody.

In a low, conspiratorial voice, Dylan said, "Let's start with Martin Viktor Koslov."

Woody raised his eyebrows, creating furrows across his formerly smooth forehead. "How do you know about Koslov?"

"He left his fingerprints in the doctor's bedroom last night."

"He's not in the FBI top ten, but Koslov is definitely on our Most Wanted list." Woody shuddered. "Some of the murders he's committed are horrific. Beheading is the least awful. They say that he cut a man in half with a chainsaw while he was still conscious."

"Wow, how old is he?"

"In his late forties, maybe even early fifties, he's been around for a long time, considering the dangers of his profession. He has a reputation as kind of a health nut, watches his diet and runs five miles a day."

Long-distance running might come in handy for an assassin. "Any family?"

"None are mentioned in his file, which is about this thick." Woody held up his thumb and forefinger six inches apart. "We suspect his first crimes were for the Romero cartel based in Venezuela. Somebody in that group might be family. Oh, and his mother was Russian. She was killed in a bomb blast."

Dylan hadn't known about the connection with the Romero cartel. They were so famously evil that even he had heard of them. The cartel lurked like a giant spider on the web of crime in South America, but they weren't involved in oil…and oil was the motive for the kidnapping.

"I thought his mother was Saudi," Dylan said, trying to keep his question innocuous so Woody would blab even more.

"Nope, Russian. His mother's name isn't Koslov, but she's Russian."

"He's done a lot of dirty work for the sheikhs."

"Your sources are behind the times." Woody scoffed. "He hasn't been involved in the Middle East for years."

"But he's still active, right?"

"You bet, he is. Four months ago in June, Koslov was in Dallas, and he—" Woody clenched his jaw.

"You can tell me," Dylan encouraged.

"It's FBI business."

"Come on, Woody, it's the era of the internet. Everybody knows everything and has a flash photo."

"I said too much."

"I've been doing research on my own," Dylan said. "I know that Koslov has never been arrested. He's been taken into custody a couple of times, which is how his fingerprints got into the system, but never charged with a crime."

Tight-lipped, Woody turned away.

Apparently, he was done talking. Dylan's patience was all used up. "Last night, Koslov got careless. He left a fingerprint. And he let his intended victim escape. Why?"

"That's not typical." Woody said.

"Think about it," Dylan said.

"I'd appreciate if you'd keep an eye on her while I change into these scrubs. You're armed, aren't you?"

"Always." He darted a nervous peek down the hallway. "Do you think Koslov would come after her in the hospital?"

"Would the horrific assassin take on a bunch of unarmed civilians? The only thing stopping him is you and me." Dylan pointed toward the operating theater. "If she goes anywhere, you follow. I'll be back in ten."

He would have preferred having Mason as his backup, but Woody could probably handle a short stint of Jayne-watching. Also, Dylan had other jobs for his partner. He wanted Mason to check them out of the hotel and to stop by Jayne's place and pack at least two more outfits. After the operation, he planned to take her to a safe house, where nobody could find them. This topic wasn't up for discussion. His decision was made. It was best for her to disappear for a few days.

He ducked into a supply closet and switched into the light blue scrubs, the same color as Jayne's. He positioned one of his guns, the Glock 17, under his armpit with a body harness. His second weapon was in an ankle holster.

When he returned to the OR, he found Woody standing where he was supposed to in the observation area. As soon as Dylan joined him, the FBI agent complained, "I'm hungry."

"When you go for lunch, there's something I want you to check."

"Now you're giving me orders."

While Woody launched into a monologue about how the FBI deserved more respect, Dylan peered through the window and focused on Jayne. The blue in her scrubs and in her cap brought out the color of her eyes.

For a moment, she looked right at him, caught his gaze, and he felt a tug that drew him toward her.

Aware that Woody had stopped talking, Dylan shrugged. "Okay, fine. I won't tell you my lead."

"I didn't say I wouldn't help you. Go ahead."

Dylan went through the deductive reasoning that made him believe Koslov had used a hacker to disable Jayne's alarm system. "I checked some of our local computer experts and found that Tank Sherman seems to be on the move. He's trying to hide."

"Because Tank did a job for Koslov, and Koslov doesn't leave loose ends." Woody nodded. "I'm going to lunch, and I'll track down these loose ends later."

Dylan watched him go, figuring that he wouldn't see Woody for at least two hours.

Though the patient wasn't yet in the OR, there were seven people, including Jayne, in the room. All wore scrubs, caps and throwaway gloves. Nobody had on a mask. None of them looked in the least bit suspicious.

Jayne popped her head into the outer area. "Dylan, why don't you scrub up, put on some gloves and come in here."

With all the cool machines? She didn't need to ask twice. In the operating room, she waved him over and introduced him to the nurses, another surgeon and a neurologist who seemed to share his raging fascination with the equipment. The atmosphere was friendly and relaxed, but Jayne was clearly in charge. Not bossy—these people were her peers. She was genuinely more comfortable than he'd ever imagined she could be. No wonder she insisted on staying here. For Jayne, this was home.

Listening to the neurologist, Dylan picked up enough of the technical specs and data to generally comprehend how these machines worked. Some of the hospital equipment was dedicated to keeping the patient alive during the procedure. Others monitored and displayed. The shiny chrome superstars of technology were designed to mimic the interconnectivity of nerve endings. He particularly liked the brain-wave measurements on the oscilloscope.

Jayne appeared at his side. "What do you think?"

He gazed down at the neuron design on her surgical cap. Her brain, he suspected, was beautiful. "Impressive."

"And now, all we need is the patient."

"Do you bring him in here before you knock him out?"

"He's not unconscious," she said. "The anesthesiologist has to numb the physical pain while keeping the patient awake. It's a difficult procedure."

It all sounded difficult to him but also interesting. "I'd like to come here another time, when we don't have anything else to worry about."

"That can be arranged. What happened to your little fed friend?"

"Lunch break."

"That figures," she said dismissively. "He seemed

like the type who would be more concerned with filling his belly than learning something."

Not like me. He waited for her to pat him on the back for taking an intelligent interest in the process, but she was already talking to the neurologist about a complex procedure involving the subthalamic nucleus. Jayne wasn't the type of person who scattered compliments like confetti.

He wanted her to notice him…in a positive way. He felt the words crawling up his throat and did his best to tamp them down. It was no use. He spoke up, "It's only a matter of time, you know, before the computer experts and the medical experts get together and invent a machine that can do neurosurgery."

Her full, pink lips flattened in a cold smile. "Then I'll be out of a job."

"Not what I meant," he said.

"I know."

They'd spoken these words before, but it was the other way around. Dylan thought he knew her deeply, that he recognized the Jayne under the facade. Surprise, surprise, he wasn't the only one with X-ray vision. She understood his need to appear cool and smart, not unusual for a nerd.

She took his arm. "Let me show you around before my patient arrives."

They went through the swinging doors and down a corridor wide enough for gurneys, and then she took a left at a short dead-end hallway that led to a break room.

Just outside were bathrooms. Though Dylan's trained eyes were constantly on the lookout for any threat, he found himself focusing on the gentle touch of her hand on his arm.

Thrusting out his free arm in a disjointed gesture, he pointed to the ladies' room. "We should talk about bathroom breaks. I should enter before you and make sure nobody is hiding inside."

Not paying attention, she nodded, dropping his arm as she strode through the empty break room. Much of the color scheme in the hospital was typical Southwestern colors, like turquoise, gold and terra-cotta red. In the break room, the colors were deeper, with an added purple and a red the color of chili peppers. Not exactly soothing after a long surgery, the loud colors might be why the room was empty. She stood before the vending machine, contemplating the choices. "I should probably eat something."

He wanted to feed her a lavish gourmet meal and watch her eat, chewing slowly. All that appeared to be available were a variety of candy bars, snack cakes and chips. "I could go down to the cafeteria. Well, I wouldn't go myself because I need to stay with you, but I could get someone else to…"

She turned and faced him. Before he could activate his lightning-quick reflexes, she went up on her toes and kissed him on the cheek. Then she turned back to the vending machine. Over her shoulder, she said, "Couldn't help it. You're cute when you get befuddled."

He was willing to concede that she was smarter than he was…and probably a better leader…and, very likely, she was more confident. But he wasn't about to let her take the lead when it came to what happened between them.

He was the bodyguard. He was in charge.

He grasped her upper arm and spun her around to face him. Holding her other arm to anchor her to one spot in the empty break room, he kissed her. Not a belittling peck on the cheek, but a real kiss on the lips. His mouth pressed firmly against hers, he tasted mint and coffee. Though their bodies weren't touching, the heat that radiated between them was hotter than a furnace.

When her arms tugged to be free, he mentally prepared to be slapped. But she didn't end the kiss after he released her. Her slender arms encircled his neck. Her body joined with his, and her tongue plunged into his mouth. Entwined together, they maneuvered past chairs and tables until he had her pressed against the chili-red wall. His tongue probed her lips, and she opened her mouth, welcoming him inside.

For the first time since they'd met, Dylan and Jayne were in complete agreement.

Chapter Seven

Jayne reveled in the physical sensations that his kiss activated in her body. Every nerve ending trembled with excitement. Her limbic system was on fire, and the dopamine was flowing. She was overwhelmed by sensation.

All the intelligence sapped out of her as she wrapped her left leg around him and felt his erection pushing against her abdomen. It had probably been two months ago that she'd been on a date and been held by a man. But those caresses hadn't felt like this. That date had been the very definition of *who cares*?

Dylan's kiss was something far different. It consumed her. There was probably a solid neurological explanation for why she was swept up in tremors of ecstasy. But she didn't care.

A low moan of pleasure escaped her lips. So inappropriate, that they were doing this in the break room next to the stale chips and wretched coffee. She needed to stop. *Right now*, she told herself. *Or in a minute*.

As if reading her mind, he separated his mouth from

hers and gazed down at her. When he reached up to straighten his glasses, he instead removed them. His unshielded gaze focused intently upon her. Reverting to her true identity as a neurosurgeon, she noted that his pupils were so dilated she could barely see the gray of the iris—a clear sign of attraction.

Proudly she smiled. She'd done that to him. He was so thoroughly turned-on that his eyes were solid black and his erection was rock solid. She had done it, and it felt good.

"What's funny?" he asked.

"I am." She shrugged. "And you are."

Jayne hadn't planned to kiss him. From the first time she'd seen him, she'd thought he was oddly attractive, but she wasn't looking for a mate, unlike the OR nurse who'd taken one peek at Dylan and asked if he was single. Was that why she'd kissed him? To put her mark on him and let other women know he was taken?

A silence stretched between them. Not because they were uncomfortable. They didn't need words to communicate.

She took a backward step. Without speaking, she was telling him that they needed to get moving. The time for the operation was nigh. She didn't release his hand—another silent communication. She wanted to stay connected to him.

He squeezed her fingertips, asserting his dominance. She squeezed back lightly, letting him know that she wasn't a total pushover and deciding that she was reading far too much into minor gestures.

Returning to reality, she said, "There's someone I want you to meet."

"Sure." When he put his glasses back on, their moment was over. "Lead the way."

She made the walk down the long corridor that led to one of the waiting rooms for the friends and family of surgical patients. Though her hypothalamus was still doing a happy dance, certain memories sobered her mood. This was the walk she took to inform those waiting of the results. There were six times in the eight years when she'd been in charge of the surgeries that she'd had to deliver bad news. She remembered each of those patients and their families. Even now, their names and faces resurfaced in her mind. She and her team had tried their hardest to save them, but their best wasn't enough.

She was glad that her memory-stimulation surgery—the procedure on the agenda for today—wasn't life threatening unless some terrible accident occurred, something like a power outage or mislabeled anesthetic. She wasn't careless about the operation: all surgery was dangerous. But her outcomes on memory stimulation, except for one man who certainly wasn't made worse by her surgery, had been a parade of successes.

By the time they got to the waiting room, Jayne was smiling. The next time she made this walk, she would have good news. Seated in the corner with a very large backpack at her feet and a book in her hand was Cordelia Cameron, the wife of the professor who was Jayne's patient. The small woman with graying hair fastened in a chignon at her nape greeted the surgeon with a big hug.

When Jayne introduced Dylan, Mrs. Cameron cocked her head to one side and looked up at him. "Are you the man who answered my phone call this morning?"

"Yes, ma'am."

She went up on tiptoe to hug him, too. "I'm so glad Jayne finally has a boyfriend. Are you a doctor?"

"He's in computers," Jayne said quickly.

Mrs. Cameron returned to her chair. "My goodness, Dylan, you're a big one, aren't you?"

"I am," he said.

"And I'll bet you're hungry." She unzipped the top of her backpack and took out a round plastic container. Inside were fresh-baked goodies. "Jayne is always half-starved, and she really likes my chocolate chip cookies."

Dylan accepted a treat. "You asked about cookies this morning."

"This container is for you two. I have another for Henry." She continued to dig through the backpack.

Though Jayne hadn't expected food, she was salivating. "What else have you got there, Mrs. Cameron?"

"You told me that the operation would take five or six hours, and I've eaten in the hospital cafeteria more than once. It is not a delight. I made some sandwiches for me and some extra for you. Tuna salad, ham or peanut butter?"

"I have a few things I wanted to explain before I started to operate." In the past, Mrs. Cameron had been interested in hearing about the procedure. "Why don't we take your yummy backpack and go into one of these conference rooms?"

Jayne led the way back into the corridor and opened the door to a small room with windows along one wall. The plants and soft pastel green-and-yellow walls did their best to make this simple space with a sofa, a round table and a few chairs seem comforting to those who waited. Jayne preferred the loud purple and red in the break room, but that area was reserved for the hospital staff.

While tearing into a tuna sandwich, she ran through the basic tests that had already been performed on Henry Cameron, professor emeritus at University of Denver. "The MRIs and CAT scans are clear. His blood work didn't show any new or unusual problems. Pressure is good. I can tell that you've been watching his diet and keeping him healthy."

"You bet I am." Her small hand clenched in a tight, determined fist. She wasn't about to let her husband go. "His cardiologist says his heart is doing fine after the bypass."

"And he's able to walk without assistance?"

"He's capable of getting out and about as much as

he was before the heart attack," Mrs. Cameron said, "but he doesn't want to go anywhere. He's depressed."

"About his memory loss."

Jayne ate the sandwich, sipped water from a bottle that Mrs. Cameron produced from her ubiquitous backpack and listened as the concerned lady described her husband's frustration with being unable to recognize old friends or students. He couldn't recall lessons he'd taught for forty years, and when he started reading up on them again, he was angry with himself for forgetting such simple truths. The worst thing about being very smart was that you noticed the gaps when you forgot.

Professor Cameron was the perfect candidate for her memory-stimulation surgery. Apart from the brain issues, his health was good. And he was motivated, eager to regain what he had lost.

"As I've told you before," Jayne said, "there's very little risk with this procedure, and your husband will be awake most of the time. After attaching electrodes, we start by drilling two holes in the skull."

She noticed Dylan leaning forward in his chair and listening, showing a real interest. "Excuse me," he said. "Why do you need two holes?"

Jayne looked toward Mrs. Cameron. "Do you want to tell him?"

"One is for the right side," she said, "and another for the left. I think I understand, Jayne. After you make the holes, you send in a probe to find exactly the right spot, and then you implant a microelectrode, which is as tiny as a human hair, to stimulate memory."

The description sounded so very simple. It seemed crazy that it had taken vast improvements in technology to provide the equipment needed and countless hours on her part to perfect her technique. "Essentially, that's all."

"When will we know if it worked?" Mrs. Cameron asked.

"Right away. Henry will be talking throughout."

Dylan asked, "What about the anesthesia? It'll take him a while to recover from that."

"It's a light dose," Jayne said. "Similar to the lidocaine used by your dentist."

His expression of disbelief was comical. "And it doesn't hurt?"

"The brain itself doesn't feel pain," she said. "There are many complicated explanations of this issue. Suffice it to say, I can cut into a naked brain, and the subject won't experience discomfort."

"How is that possible?" he asked.

"Pain is a warning system. If you touch a flame, the pain tells you to move your hand. If the brain is injured, the warning has come too late."

Jayne didn't want to get too graphic about what happens, not with the wife of her patient listening. But she'd heard of cases where an individual with an exposed brain could walk about and speak coherently.

"I have another question," Mrs. Cameron said.

"When you're done with Henry, will you say something to him for me?"

"Of course."

The older woman's eyes filled with tears as she spoke, "It's a quote. 'Shall I compare thee to a summer's day?' He used to recite that sonnet to me. If he remembers, I'll feel like he has truly come back to me."

Jayne gave her hand a squeeze and went toward the OR, where Henry was being prepped.

AFTER THE FIRST two hours of the procedure, Dylan leaned back in his seat in the gallery, looked away from the OR and checked his cell phone. There were two text messages from Detective Cisneros.

The first read, PS cut back on his Mid-East biz. No current enemies. Unlikely terrorism. The initials "PS" must refer to Peter Shackleford, and "no current enemies" indicated that Jayne's father hadn't ticked off anybody in the Middle East, not lately. Cisneros had to be pleased that the threat to Jayne didn't involve terrorism…just an assassin with a ruthless sensibility.

The second message: PS talked to source in Mid-East. Koslov not working for his usual employers.

Dylan sent back a text telling the detective that the feds were on the case, and Agent Woody was looking into their hacker. He also noted the link between Koslov and the Romero cartel and suggested Cisneros question Jayne's dad to find out if he'd managed to irritate Diego

Romero, the most bloodthirsty drug lord in Venezuela. Then he turned off the phone again.

He looked down the row of chairs to where Woody was sitting. The FBI agent had returned to the hospital about an hour and a half ago with his wardrobe changed to his typical dark suit, white shirt and dark blue necktie. He didn't need to produce a badge—Woody was a walking advertisement for the feds.

Now might be a good time for a chat with him, not that Dylan was in any way bored as he sat in the gallery among students and docs. A short man with a little potbelly pushing against the front of his dark blue scrubs gave a running commentary of what was happening. It was "amygdala" this and "hypothalamus" that. One of the nurses referred to him as a "neurogroupie" who liked to pretend that someday he'd grow up and be a surgeon.

Dylan appreciated the play-by-play commentary. He was fascinated when they drilled the holes into Henry Cameron's skull. As Jayne had promised, there wasn't much blood. And there were nurses who seemed to have the sole job of suctioning away anything that might be messy.

Every person in the operating room wore a sterile gown and cap over the scrubs. Even in that shapeless outfit with a mask covering her mouth and special goggles, Jayne was hot. He remembered how her firm, slender body had molded to his torso when she'd kissed him back and wrapped her leg around him.

In the operating room, she was definitely in charge. The other docs, even a guy who was clearly her senior, deferred to her judgment and followed her orders. She had wakened Henry from his light sleep and was talking to him...while he had holes in his head. There were constant bleeps from some of the stainless-steel electronics. The screens with imaging of the brain showed precisely what happened when Jayne probed in different areas.

After two-and-a-half hours, they still hadn't finished with the left side. He signaled to Woody and they stepped away from the others for a private talk. Once again near the nurses' station, Dylan positioned himself so he was able to see every approach to Operating Room 1A.

Dylan spoke first. "What did you find out about Tank?"

"Nobody's seen the kid since yesterday afternoon." Woody shot a furtive gaze down the hallway. "My people tracked his laptop to an abandoned house in the foothills. No sign of Tank. He had removed the computer's memory and destroyed it."

"But he left the tracking system intact?" That made no sense whatsoever...unless Tank wanted them to find some kind of evidence. "What else did he leave at this house?"

"Nothing," Woody said. "Are you sure he was the one who did the hack?"

"I'm sure." He'd explained once already. He had discovered digital evidence that the kid had hacked into Jayne's security system last night and disabled it. Dylan's fingers were itching to get onto a keyboard and find answers for himself. "I hope Tank is okay."

"He's a criminal. These hackers don't deserve sympathy."

Spoken like a heartless fed. "Have your guys unearthed any news about the Romero cartel? Any reason they might want to get revenge on Jayne's father?"

"They've been quiet, lately. The old man, Diego Romero, hasn't been well. He's an evil bastard and so are his men. I don't know why they'd go outside the cartel to find an assassin."

"Kidnapping takes more finesse."

"Maybe so."

"I need to check in with my partner. I'd appreciate if you could stay here and keep an eye on Jayne for fifteen minutes."

"I owe you for the tip on Tank Sherman. Take your time. I'm going to be here until she's done."

As if on cue, Jayne stepped into the hallway. She'd already slipped out of the bundle of sterile clothes that covered her. Another doctor—the gray-haired man—joined her.

In an instant, Dylan was beside her. He kept his voice low. "Is everything all right?"

"It's great," she said. After two-and-a-half hours of meticulous surgery, he expected her to be tired or stressed. It was the opposite. Energy crackled around her. This woman loved her job. "The patient is responding beautifully. I've finished my work on the left side."

The doctor accompanying her said, "We needed a break before moving to the next phase."

"More food?" Dylan offered. "Water?"

"I've been staying hydrated," she said. "Maybe a bit too well hydrated. I'm out here for a bathroom break."

He fell into step beside her, leaving Woody and the other doctor standing in the corridor outside the OR. Escorting clients to the toilet was *not* one of Dylan's favorite things. When they got to the door, he stepped in front of her and pulled his handgun.

"This will just take a minute." He pushed open the door to the ladies' restroom and yelled, "Anybody in here?"

His voice echoed off the tiled walls. The room with three stalls seemed empty, but he wasn't taking any chance. He whisked her inside, and then he searched each stall. Avoiding her gaze, he held the door open.

"Um, thanks," she murmured.

"I'll be waiting outside."

As if he couldn't feel like more of a jerk, Dylan stepped out of the ladies' room and immediately saw Jayne's father walking toward him. Peter Shackleford was accompanied by a black-haired man with heavy-lidded eyes, stubble on his jaw and a suit that looked like it had been made for him.

"Javier Flores," Jayne's dad introduced him. "His

family has been in the Venezuelan oil business for three generations."

The area outside the OR and the intensive-care unit was restricted. But Dylan had the feeling that Flores went wherever he wanted, whenever he wanted to go. He was sleek and intense. His dark eyes held unreadable secrets, and there was an edge about him. This was a mature and formidable man. Dylan needed to keep his eye on Flores.

Chapter Eight

After exchanging polite greetings with the Venezuelan, Dylan glanced toward Peter and said, "Jayne will be happy that you're here."

"Why?"

"You'll be able to watch the rest of the surgery she's performing."

Peter blinked as though he'd just awakened and found himself in a hospital corridor. "Surgery?"

"The procedure she created," Dylan said, reminding him. "She's able to stimulate memory in stroke victims."

"Fascinating," Flores said. "I did not know your daughter was a brain surgeon. Is this procedure successful?"

"Very much so," Dylan said.

Jayne emerged from the restroom and confronted them. Her gaze rested on her father. Dylan knew she was looking for a sign of acknowledgment from Peter the Great. In the medical community, she received a ton of recognition. She was a superstar. But she still wanted applause from her father.

Peter came toward her. "I hope we're not too late to watch you do your thing."

"My thing?" Her eyes narrowed suspiciously.

"Implanting the memory electrode," Flores said as he shook her hand and introduced himself to Jayne. Dylan hadn't mentioned electrodes or implants. How did Flores know?

Her father asked, "When will you be finished?"

"About another hour or hour and a half."

"Afterward," Flores said, "we must take you out for an early dinner to celebrate another success."

Dylan's protective instincts came to the forefront as he watched the handsome, perfectly tailored Venezuelan oozing charm all over Jayne. Was Flores naturally gushy around women? Drawn to Jayne in particular? Or did he have a more nefarious motive?

Dylan was glad when she turned to him and asked, "What do you think about dining out?"

The standard policy at TST Security was to allow clients to set their own agenda and then work around them. But Jayne wasn't a standard client...not after that kiss in the break room. Dylan didn't trust himself to stand by silently and observe while she was wined and dined. "We might need to take you to a safe house."

To Flores, she said, "We'll talk later. Now I need to get back to surgery."

As she returned to the area where she would wash up and don her sterile gear before entering OR 1A, Dylan took her dad and Flores to the seating area nearby. "You can observe from here."

"An hour and a half longer," her dad muttered. "You know, the procedure is already under way. We probably won't understand a thing."

"No problem," Dylan said as he introduced Jayne's father to the talkative groupie. The chatty observer in the dark blue scrubs was delighted to meet the father of the brilliant Dr. Shackleford and equally pleased to have a fresh audience.

Dylan pulled Flores to one side and asked, "What can you tell me about Martin Viktor Koslov?"

"Vermin." His lip curled in a sneer. "If you had not found a fingerprint, I would never believe this was the work of Martin Koslov. To disable the alarm is like him, but I have never known him to allow a victim to escape. Why would Koslov be hired for a kidnapping?"

"His employer might be someone he's worked for on a regular basis," Dylan suggested, "someone from his home country."

"He was born in Venezuela, but I hate to claim him as one of my countrymen." Flores clenched his fist as though he could strangle bad influences. "Koslov comes from the dark underbelly of my culture and represents the worst atrocities."

Dylan pushed for a more specific answer. "I've heard that Koslov is linked to the Romero cartel."

"More than a link," Flores said in a low voice.

"Koslov is rumored to be the bastard son of Diego Romero himself."

According to the information Dylan had unearthed, Koslov lost his father when he was very young and was raised by his Russian mother in Caracas until he was eleven. Then she was killed in a street explosion, and he was taken in by another family. "My information about his parents is vague, except for the detail that his mother was Russian."

"A stunning woman, she played the violin and sang in a nightclub in Caracas. Diego Romero could not resist this exotic flower. He took her as his mistress, leaving his wife and his other three children behind in their village. When she was killed, Martin Koslov was bounced back and forth between the Russian consulate and an aunt of Diego Romero."

Quite an elaborate backstory for an assassin, and Dylan took it with a grain of salt. "Do you think Koslov is working for the cartel?"

"The old man has been unwell, certainly not strong enough to launch an attack against Peter. What would be gained by such an assault? Romero has nothing to do with the oil business."

"Are you sure he's not branching out?"

"Oil is the business of my family." His gaze was as dark and hard as anthracite. "I know nothing of a threat against Peter, surely not a tactic that involved the abduction of his daughter the doctor."

If Flores was lying, he was doing a good job of it.

When he'd heard that Jane was a brain surgeon, he'd seemed honestly surprised and impressed with her skill. And he definitely wasn't the type to hold Jayne in a kidnapping.

Dylan directed him toward the seating where Peter the Great was being lectured by the chatty man in scrubs who seemed to know more about Jayne's procedure than she did. Peering through the glass, Dylan observed her delicate expertise as she continued the surgery. He wished he could gather her up, wrapped in her sterile gown and mask, and whisk her away to safety.

JAYNE GAVE HER full concentration to the procedure, posing questions to Professor Henry Cameron about lessons he'd taught many years ago and then asking what he'd had for breakfast this morning. A problem arose when Henry tried to translate his memories into language, and she dealt with that aspect, smoothing it over as best she could. The recovery of memory wasn't an exact science, not yet anyway, and she warned her patients not to expect perfection.

In the back of her mind, she was aware of her dad showing up to watch her surgery. Would he stick around for the whole thing? She hoped so. His approval was important to her. He'd never been disparaging, but his enthusiasm for her career in neurosurgery was at the same level as when his third wife's Yorkie won second prize at a kennel club show. Actually, he was more excited about the pooch. She wanted those pats on the head, wanted to be stroked and told that she was a good girl.

The wounds on Henry's head were closed when she removed the brace from his jaw and forehead, allowing him to move more freely. His wide grin filled her with hope and joy.

"Better?" she asked.

"So much better. Thank you, Jayne."

"Your wife asked if I would say something to you when the operation ended." She cleared her throat and quoted Shakespeare. "'Shall I compare thee to a summer's day?'"

"Here's what you tell her," he said. "'Thou art more lovely and more temperate.'"

Tears prickled the backs of her eyelids. Her priorities adjusted themselves. This successful procedure would help Henry and his wife have a better, more meaningful life. That success was what gave Jayne satisfaction. She hadn't become a neurosurgeon to prove anything to herself or to impress her father. She was a doctor. She was in the business of helping.

As Henry was wheeled away into ICU, she peeled off the sterile garb and got down to her scrubs. She left the OR, glanced at the observation area and didn't see her father. Had he left? Already? Dylan was down the hall, talking to Detective Cisneros.

She didn't want to lose the joy she felt at the successful operation. Waving to Dylan, she said, "I'm going down the hall to talk to Henry's wife."

"Wait," he said.

She kept going. After she delivered her sweet Shakespearean message to Mrs. Cameron, she'd hurry back to the OR and find out where her father had gone. She couldn't believe he'd left, not after his friend had offered a celebratory dinner.

Arms swinging, she passed the brightly colored break room where she and Dylan had kissed. Halfway down the hall, she went by the door to the room where she'd earlier talked to Mrs. Cameron. In the waiting room, she saw the backpack, but Henry's wife wasn't sitting beside it. There was only one other person in the waiting area, a haggard blonde woman who slouched over in a row of chairs.

Jayne approached the blonde and asked, "Excuse me, have you seen the lady who was sitting in this corner?"

"Bathroom," she mumbled. Her eyelids slammed shut.

Jayne was aware of someone coming up behind her. Dylan? Before she could turn to face him, she felt a pinch on her thigh as though she'd been given a shot. A masculine arm coiled across her waist. A low voice whispered, "Come with me, Jayne."

She recognized the accent.

It was the guy from last night. Martin Viktor Koslov had found her, caught her. His callused hand clamped over her mouth.

Frantic, she jerked her forearm back, aiming for his face and hitting nothing but air as he easily avoided her blow. She drove her elbow back sharply and hit his rock-hard rib cage. *I have to get away from him, have to run.* Hopping from one foot to the other, she tried to counter-balance and wrench herself from his grasp, but he held her arms, pinned her backside against his chest as he yanked her away from the woman whose eyes were still closed. How could that lady just sit there? She must have heard the struggle. *Open your eyes, lady, help me.*

Instead, the woman deliberately turned away and hunched her shoulder.

Help me, help me! Jayne twisted her head so she could scream. His hand stayed over her mouth, muffling her attempt to make noise. Her strength was waning. Whatever he'd given her in that shot was taking effect. She wouldn't give up. *Not without a fight.* She opened her jaw and chomped down hard on the fleshy pad of his hand.

He growled a feral curse, spun her to face him. She took note of his surgical mask and cap, keeping the lower part of his face covered like it was last night. He smacked her hard, a fierce backhand that caused her head to snap back.

She actually saw stars, pinpoints of light against a black velvet curtain that threatened to fall and blank out her mind.

Though reeling from the blow, she opened her mouth to scream. Her lips stuck to her teeth. Her throat was dry. No sound came through her lips. *Losing control, I'm losing control.* She wanted to fight, but she couldn't.

Where was Dylan? He was her bodyguard. He was supposed to prevent this sort of thing. It felt like she'd been struggling for hours, but she knew it was only a few minutes since Koslov had plunged a hypodermic into her thigh, probably something like chloral hydrate or ketamine, knockout drops.

Her knees weakened. She braced herself against the back of a chair to keep from falling. *Which way is up? Which is down?* The room was spinning around her. Dizzy, disoriented, clumsy, she stumbled a few paces and sank into the wheelchair he held for her.

He pulled down the footrests and whispered, "Don't try to move. Don't make a sound. I'm not going to hurt you."

She didn't think she would have recognized him. Not with the mask. Not in those dark blue scrubs. Half the people in this building were in scrubs. They looked alike, all alike.

"Jayne?"

She swung her head toward the sound of her name. It was Mrs. Cameron coming out of the restroom. Far away, she was so far away. Jayne didn't want to frighten the woman. She tried to smile, tried to tell her that her husband had given the correct response. "'Thou art more lovely and more temperate.'" Jayne spoke the words, but she knew they came out garbled.

Before she could explain, Koslov whisked her away. He propelled the wheelchair toward the elevators. She tried to sit up straight, tried to move her legs and tumble from the chair. Her head felt unwieldy and heavy. With a sigh, she let her chin loll forward onto her chest.

She forced her eyes to open, saw Dylan running toward her. *Too late, he's too late.* Her last conscious thought was that she might never get to kiss him again.

And that would be a damn shame.

Chapter Nine

Even before she awakened, Jayne knew she wasn't at
home in her comfy bed with the adjustable firmness
and Egyptian-cotton linens. There was a strange aroma.
Her nostrils flared as she inhaled a long, deep breath
of freshness and nature. She sneezed and groaned. The
bedsprings creaked as she burrowed deeper under the
heavy pile of blankets.

Some people liked earthy smells, which she'd never
been able to comprehend. The olfactory region in her
brain interpreted the great outdoors as stinky, causing
her to literally turn up her nose. Her favorite fragrance
was sanitary nothingness. No smell at all, or maybe a
hint of citrus.

Bemused, she imagined the map of the brain with
an orange blossom sheltering the olfactory area. Part of
the limbic system, sense of smell was connected to the
amygdala and emotion, which was why particular smells
helped recall events in the past. She inhaled, remembering the sharp pine scent of her father's aftershave.
Unexpectedly, tears oozed through her closed eyelids.

She gave herself a mental shake. *Wake up, Jayne!* Her mind was fuzzy around the edges. She had vague memories of many things, some of which didn't make sense and others that couldn't possibly be true. She was a respected neurosurgeon who never indulged in wheelchair chases through the hospital corridors. Why was she imagining such a mad dash?

There had been explosions...fireworks or gunfire or something else? And Dylan, she definitely recalled being held in Dylan's arms, snuggled against his warmth, soothed by the steady rhythm of his heartbeat.

He had told her that they were going somewhere safe. As if she could just up and leave whenever she felt like it? Deserting her patients, dismissing consultations, altogether dropping the ball? She wouldn't do that. She was, above all, responsible.

Pursing her lips, she tried to say "responsible." She pushed out each individual syllable. Then she said the full word: responsible.

Her jaw ached. When she patted her cheek lightly, she felt a wide area of tenderness on her face. There would be a bruise. Someone had hit her. Koslov!

Adrenaline flushed through her veins. She was wide-awake. Though she wasn't alert or aware of what had led to this point, she was conscious. Sitting up on the bed with the polished brass frame, she looked around with new eyes. Morning sunlight spilled around the edges of the curtains and across the warm, knotty pine paneling on the bedroom walls. She had the sense that she was in a cabin in a forest. Yes, she was sure that she'd been driven into the mountains when it was dark.

Climbing from bed, she noticed that she was wearing her own baby-blue flannel pajamas with penguins skiing across them. She didn't remember changing clothes. Had Dylan undressed her? Probably not—a man would have chosen one of her skimpy gowns instead of long-sleeved flannel, which was so practical during the chill of a September night.

She pulled open the dark burgundy curtains and stared past a thick stand of pines toward a two-story cedar house and a big red barn. A cowboy rode toward her window. It was Dylan.

The moment she recognized him, she smiled, causing a twinge in her cheek. Dylan was wearing a dark brown flat-brimmed hat, jeans and a denim shirt rolled up at the sleeves. His long hair was tucked behind his ears. He didn't have his glasses.

He sat tall in the saddle…of a camel.

Jayne widened her eyes and blinked. *Not a hallucination.* For some reason, Dylan was perched atop a Bactrian camel with two humps and a lot of fur. She couldn't recall if the coat on a camel was referred to as fur or as wool. Her father owned an overcoat of camel hair, but she'd never thought the fabric was the hair of a camel, literally.

And why was she worrying about cowboys and camels? She had more than enough problems of her own without getting involved in Dylan's weirdness. Barefoot, she stalked from the bedroom through the cozy front room of the cabin, almost tripping over a very large gray cat, and out the front door, where she stood on the porch with her arms folded below her breasts.

Dylan tapped the camel with a riding crop. After a haughty look down its long nose, the animal batted extra long eyelashes. When the camel opened its mouth, the sound was a cross between an infant's cry and squealing brakes at a ten-car pileup. Charming!

"What on earth are you doing?"

He made an introductory gesture. "This is Loretta."

"I don't care."

He reached back to pat the camel's rump. "Don't pay any attention to her, Loretta. Jayne's a grouch, but you're lovely."

She narrowed her gaze. "Have I ever told you how I hate when people have conversations with their pets?"

Loretta let out another screech.

"Now you've upset her." Dylan poked along the animal's side, giving a signal of some sort. "Get back, Loretta."

In response to his gentle prods, the beast folded its knees, first in the front and then in the back. Dylan swung his leg over the front hump, dismounted and approached the porch. In his cowboy boots, he was even taller than usual. His hat shaded his silver-eyed gaze.

Though Jayne had never been a big fan of cowboys,

with their long legs and lean torsos, Dylan looked good in that gear. He was studly enough to spark a dozen fantasies.

She was tempted to throw herself into his arms and encourage him to erase her concerns with his kisses. But she'd never been so easy to please. Jayne didn't know what was going on...and probably wasn't going to be happy about it. She held out her palm in a gesture that meant *halt*, and he obeyed.

He stood at the bottom of the four wide stairs leading to the porch. "How are you feeling?" he asked.

Not wanting to get sidetracked by symptoms, she didn't mention her aching jaw or her headache or the overall stiffness in her muscles and joints. Her body would heal. It was more important to find out what had happened.

"My last clear memory," she said, "is sitting in a wheelchair and watching an elevator door close. You were running toward me."

"I didn't make it in time," he said. "Do you know who was pushing the wheelchair?"

"Koslov." Instead of shuddering, the muscles in her shoulders tensed and her fingers drew into fists. Her fear was turning to anger. "He came up behind me and shot a hypodermic into my thigh. He kept me from screaming by covering my mouth with his hand. Then I bit him."

"You bit him?"

"That's right." She braced herself against the handrail at the edge of the porch. She closed her eyes to stimulate her auditory and olfactory memories. "He growled. His flesh smelled filthy. He tasted like salt." Her eyes opened and she saw the upper portion of his face. His eyes were dark and angry. "That's when he slapped me."

"Bastard," Dylan muttered as he reached toward her.

"Don't touch me."

"Why not?"

"I need to cling to these shreds of memory." She concentrated. "He said he didn't want to hurt me. But he shot me full of drugs. And he slapped me."

"For somebody like Koslov, those are love taps." He climbed one step higher on the stair. "He hasn't killed you. Twice, he's chosen to let you escape."

"What happened when the elevator door closed?"

"He must have gotten off quickly with you, but he punched every button going upstairs and down. That was twelve stories, and the elevator stopped on each floor. Detective Cisneros went directly to the helipad on the roof."

She didn't have any recollection of being carried away by a chopper, and it seemed like something so dramatic would make an impression, even if she was almost unconscious. "Was I in an aircraft?"

"Very likely, that was Koslov's original plan, but Cisneros was able to shut down air traffic over downtown. There was an unauthorized helo in the area of Roosevelt Hospital, but they zipped away."

"You came after me," she said.

"I ran the odds on several possible scenarios in my head." In spite of the cowboy outfit, his true nerd-like nature shone through. "Koslov needed to get you to a vehicle to escape. Because I had memorized the blueprints for the hospital and medical building, I knew the most likely escapes were the parking area and the main entrance, where a person in a wheelchair wouldn't be noticed. My brother, Sean, was nearby and I contacted him to watch the front."

"And where did you go?"

"Ran up the stairs to the second floor," he said as he took another step closer. "I backtracked the route we took from your office this morning, crossing the walkway into the medical building. The med building has an underground parking lot."

Of course, she knew about the underground lot. She used it in bad weather. "But he couldn't go there. That parking is restricted to hospital personnel."

"Koslov isn't exactly a model citizen when it comes to following the rules."

Dylan eased his boot onto the next stair. Only one stair down from the porch where she was standing, he paused. It occurred to her that he was being extremely cautious about approaching her. Had they argued?

Her excitement at seeing him was rampant and obvious, but she didn't know whether her adrenal surge was because they were feuding or because of the unexpected attraction she'd felt from the first moment they'd met.

Though the effect of the drug had almost worn off, she was still a bit off balance. Glancing at the far end of the porch, she saw two long, furry animals racing around in a circle. "What are those?"

"Ferrets," he said.

She wanted to know more about the camels and ferrets, but she wanted the rest of the story about Koslov first. "What happened when you focused on the underground parking?"

"I tried like hell to catch him in the walkway or heading toward the elevators in the building where you have your office. But the medical complex is a maze with twists and turns in strange, illogical patterns." He was speaking faster and faster. "On the blueprint in my mind, I imagined every single door that exited the building. Koslov could have taken any of them. Or even a window."

"Not a window." She pointed out, "I was in a wheelchair."

"Yeah, sure, but he could have picked you up, could have carried you. I was so damn scared that he'd get away. I kept telling myself that he needed a car. I'd catch him when he tried to get you into his vehicle."

Dylan was on the porch, talking fast. "There are three parking levels underground, and I had no way of guessing which he'd use. I needed to stop him before he exited the garage. With phone coordination from Detective Cisneros, I arranged for cop cars to quietly pull into place and block the exits."

As he spoke, she felt his energy building. He was a compelling force. She hung on his every word. "You did this while you were running through the building?"

"Cisneros did most of the contacts."

"It was your idea. You set the trap."

"But Koslov isn't a simple country mouse. This man lives for danger. He's an assassin. There were a lot of flaws in this plan."

"The wheelchair gave you an advantage," she said, getting caught up in the story. "He couldn't run, couldn't even move very fast while he was dragging me along."

"The disadvantage," Dylan said, "was also you. I didn't want to put you in danger by using my gun. And I sure as hell didn't want Koslov to get into a shoot-out with the cops outside the garage."

"If you'd been running hard on the walkway, you might have arrived at the underground parking before Koslov."

"I think, maybe, I did. There were so many variables—over twenty-seven—but only one constant," he said. "Two elevators connect the main floor with the level where you exit onto the street. Both open into the same enclosed glass area."

She added, "Don't forget the two concrete stairwells beside them."

"Actually, there are eight stairwells in different parts of the underground. Marked by Exit signs, their doors are locked, only used in emergency, which isn't an efficient use of the space if you ask me."

"Not asking." He certainly got sidetracked easily. "What happened next?"

He held her in his gaze. "Are you certain you don't remember?"

"Why do you think I might?"

"You and Koslov were talking."

She couldn't believe it. Her mouth gaped. Dylan was close enough for her to collapse into his arms, but she needed to stand on her own two feet. Pivoting, she turned and stumbled toward a wooden porch swing. A large orange-striped cat sprawled across the seat.

She pointed to the cat and then to the floor. "Move."

"You don't know much about cats, do you?"

"I know that their job is to catch small rodents. That's their place in the food chain."

"Taffy begs to differ."

"Who?"

He approached the cat and reached out to stroke the orange fur. "Good morning, Taffy. Nice, sunny day, right? Would you mind moving off the swing?"

Instead, the cat stretched out to his full length and rolled to his back, displaying his belly for petting. She was fairly certain that Dylan could chat himself blue in the face and the cat wouldn't pay the least bit of attention. "You're aware, aren't you, that you're talking to an animal?"

With an agile display of feline grace, the orange cat coiled into a ball and then stood. After parading from one end of the swing to the other, Taffy glared at her with cold, yellow eyes. Then she hopped down.

"There you go," Dylan said.

Instead of taking the seat that had been so ceremoniously vacated, she leaned her back against the smooth log wall beside the door. "You said that I had a conversation with Koslov. Explain."

"I jammed the elevator doors so they wouldn't pop open and surprise me. Then I entered one of the stairwells, moving as silently as possible. There was no one inside. As soon as I stepped into the second well, I felt a presence. Are you sure you don't recall?"

She shook her head. This was so very unlike her. She could count on one hand the number of times she hadn't been able to come up with the correct answer. The drug he'd given her had wiped her mind clean.

Dylan continued, "I heard a low murmur. Noise echoes and reverberates in those stairwells, but it seemed to be coming from below me. I looked down at the landing on the lower floor and saw you staring back at me. Your eyes were wide open. And your lips were moving. Do you remember what you said?"

Closing her eyes, she tried to access that portion of her memory. She came up blank. "I don't know."

"Koslov was behind you. He was talking. Then he whirled to face me and fired off three shots. I dodged. When I stepped back, he was gone. And you were still sitting there."

"I remember the noise," she said. The explosions

she'd heard must have been gunfire. "Were there only three shots?"

"There were a lot more. When Koslov got went into the garage, he started shooting. The cops returned fire."

"Was anyone hurt?"

"Nope, but Koslov got away clean." He gave her a warm smile. "Back in the stairwell, you were on the floor, wedged in a corner with your hands over your ears. I knelt beside you and started looking for injuries. You frowned and said, 'I am a doctor.' Then you passed out."

"I don't get it," she grumbled. "From what my dad and his friend Javier said, I expected Koslov to be a mastermind, a genius bad guy. The idea of racing through a hospital with your hostage in a wheelchair isn't exactly brilliant."

"Keep in mind that this was plan B," Dylan said. "His preferred method of escape would have been the helo on the rooftop. If Cisneros hadn't been so quick to react, Koslov would have loaded you up and flown."

Not only had the timing been lucky, but Dylan and Cisneros had done exactly the right thing at the right time. "I should send the detective a thank-you."

"I'm guessing he wouldn't say no to a bottle of Stranahan's." He pulled open the door and tried to herd her inside. "Coffee?"

But she wasn't ready to let him off the hook. "I still have more questions. You're trying to divert my attention with the offer of caffeine, and I don't appreciate your methods."

"I'm having coffee." He shrugged and went inside. "Stay out here if you want or come inside with your questions."

"I need an explanation about Loretta. Why is she here?"

"Does it really matter?"

"Yes." She stared at the beast, who sat watching through impossibly thick, long eyelashes. "If there's one thing more obvious than an elephant in the room, it's a camel by the cabin."

Chapter Ten

Dylan seldom brought guests to the RSQ Ranch. He'd designed this place as somewhere he could go to escape. Only his brother, Sean, knew the precise location, which was lucky because he'd needed Sean for backup while he drove Jayne halfway across the state to the Upper Arkansas River Valley. A beautiful location, he'd purchased this acreage near Buena Vista in the forested land above the river when he was eighteen.

He left his hat on a hook by the door. His boot heels clunked on the hard wood floor as he crossed the front room of the cabin. He didn't use the kitchen for much more than making coffee or boiling water. Usually, he grabbed his meals at the main house, where the caretakers—Betty and Tom Burton—lived full-time and housed the other occasional part-timers they needed when the ranch got busy. Dylan kept this cabin private—it was his sanctuary.

Glancing over his shoulder at Jayne, who looked cute in her penguin pajamas, he came to a realization. "I've never brought a woman here before. You're my first."

"The camel, Dylan… Tell me why there's a camel sitting in front of the cabin."

"Loretta got sick, and her owners couldn't provide the care she needed. We took her in."

She followed him into the kitchen. "Why?"

"That's what we do. RSQ Ranch is a home for animals that are old or retired or sick or no longer wanted. RSQ stands for rescue."

"Only if you can't spell." But the heavily etched frown lines between her eyebrows smoothed, and she almost smiled.

As he filled the coffeemaker with cool spring water from the tap, he explained the philosophy of the RSQ Ranch.

"We find homes for them, and we have the facilities to handle large animals. Most of our referrals come from vets or zoos. We get a lot of exotic animals…an orangutan, a pair of ocelots, an albino python, and we even have a giraffe right now."

"Why on earth would someone get rid of a giraffe?"

"She's pregnant."

He set the coffee to brew and turned toward her. She'd taken a seat at the round wooden table between the kitchen and front room. Her dark brown hair fell loosely around her face but didn't hide the swollen bruise on her right cheek.

Her vitality was starting to return. Though he still didn't see the vivacious doctor who performed surgery in the hospital, he could tell that she was almost back to normal. The haziness that had clouded her eyes was gone as she looked up at him and said, "You keep saying 'we.' Almost as though you're a part of this rescue operation."

"I own it."

"But you're a bodyguard," she said.

"Being a bodyguard is one thing I do. RSQ Ranch is another."

"You're a hard man to figure out. When we met at my neighbor's house, you looked like a nerd. At the hospital, you pulled off the professor look. And now, you're a cowboy and maybe a zookeeper."

"Tip of the iceberg," he said. "My skill sets are many and varied."

Her blue eyes glimmered as she looked up at him through her thick lashes...not as thick as the camel's, but thick. "I had a taste of another of your skill set in the break room."

A reference to their kiss. Was she flirting with him? That seemed to be the obvious conclusion. At least, he hoped it was.

He cleared his throat. Dylan had never been good at reading signals from women. Should he come right out and ask her? Grab her and kiss her? "There are a few skills you could help me with."

His face prickled with hot embarrassment. Nerd! He just didn't have the knack.

"After I've had coffee," she purred, "we can go back

into the bedroom. For now, tell me about when you were a kid."

"Like you, I was kind of a prodigy."

This story, he'd told a million times.

His genius moment had come when he got into computer games in a big way. His best friend, Mason Steele, would let him come over and play on prototypes that Mason's dad, a software designer, was developing. Long story short: Dylan created the circuitry, coding, artwork and stories for several original games. With help from Mason's dad, he sold his products and made a ton of money. The ongoing royalties were enough to keep RSQ Ranch in operation.

The fragrance of brewing coffee wafted through the kitchen. He took two ceramic mugs down from the shelf beside the sink and found a container of milk in the fridge. He held it up. "I know you prefer cream and no sugar, but all I have is milk."

"That's fine. Why aren't you wearing your glasses?"

"I lost them while I was chasing after Koslov. I've got in my contacts." He poured their coffee and placed both mugs on the table. Sitting across from her, he fought the urge to reach out and brush a wisp of hair off her face. The bruise made her features lopsided, but she was still lovely. He asked, "Are you done with the questions?"

"I've barely started." She sipped from the mug and gave a nod to indicate the coffee-to-milk ratio was all right. "Back to the story. We were in the parking garage and…"

"Koslov was on the run. I don't know how he got through all those cops, but he did."

"And you took care of me."

"I carried you into the elevator. On the main floor, I snagged a wheelchair, sat you in it and took you to the front entrance where my brother was waiting. We got into his SUV. I made the decision that you needed to be at a safe house."

"You decided." She growled. "Without consulting me, you decided?"

"You were pretty much unconscious."

"What does that mean?" she demanded. "Either I was conscious or I wasn't."

"Drooling," he said. "You didn't look like somebody I'd call in for a consultation."

"Did you even try to talk to me?"

"Actually," he said, "my number-one concern was your medical condition. Lucky for us, you're best buddies with the top brain surgeons in the world. I put in a call to Dr. Napoli, and he arranged to check you out."

"Napoli is acceptable," she said. "Not brilliant, but not bad. What did he say?"

"I recorded it."

He took his cell phone from his pocket and played back the doctor's examination. It didn't take a genius to figure out that she'd been drugged. While Napoli had her blood tested to make sure the drug wasn't lethal, he applied a cold compress to her cheek. Napoli had a lot to say about how the bruise probably didn't indicate concussion. Dylan skipped to the lab results about the drug that was used.

As soon as she heard the multisyllable name, she shrugged and said, "Not life threatening."

"Napoli gave permission allowing you to travel. I promised to keep you quiet, loaded you into the passenger seat, put on the seat belt and reclined it so you could nap."

"And we came here," she said.

"After some evasive driving to make sure Koslov wasn't on our tail."

She touched the collar of her pajamas. "How did my clothes get here?"

"My brother, Sean, went to your house and packed up a ton of stuff. Sean discovered that Koslov or his men were watching your house, and he led them on a crazy chase all over town. He made damn sure that he lost them before he came here."

"And how did I get changed?"

A memory of silk and satin undies flashed across his mind.

"Betty and Tom Burton live here full-time. Betty unpacked your clothes and got you ready for bed. She whipped up some kind of lotion for your bruise that smelled like weeds and grease."

"And then?"

"You drifted off to la-la land. I went to bed in the other room in this cabin so I could keep an eye on you."

Last night, he'd watched her sleep, synchronized his

breathing with the slow rise and fall of her chest. The cool temperature in the cabin made him think of a quiet morning under the covers with fresh sunlight pouring through the windows. "Are you about done with that coffee?"

"Are you sure we're safe?"

"Nobody knows about this place."

"Clearly, that's not true," she said. "People involved with rescues come back and forth to drop off animals. And there's the couple who live here, the Burtons."

"Nobody but my brother would connect the Dylan who lives in Denver with the Dylan who occasionally shows up at RSQ." He rose from the table and stalked into the front room. "This is the place I come to escape."

"Escape from what?"

He shook his head. "My mind gets overloaded. I'm sure you know what I mean. A psychiatrist told me it happens to smart people."

His life wasn't deeply stressful or problematic. He and his family were in good health. He liked working at TST Security. But there were times when it felt like the world was too much. There was too much noise, constant noise, overwhelming bursts of colors and activity, more than the inside of a kaleidoscope. Sometimes, he wanted to stick his nose into the sand to block the multitude of smells.

"Everybody needs an escape," she said in a soft, husky tone.

"What do you do?"

She glided her fingers down the front of his shirt. "I like to get so deeply involved in a project that the rest of the world fades away."

"Like redecorating your house," he said, "and ending up with more bathrooms than bedrooms on one small floor."

"I like getting lost in an opera. Or reading a great book from cover to cover."

Her words were innocent, but her hands were signaling a different story. She tangled her fingers in his hair, pulled his face closer to hers and kissed him.

This marked the second time that she'd initiated contact. He wanted to be the aggressor but not too aggressive or too demanding. There should be an easier protocol for physical contact, clear indications of when a kiss was enough.

The answer to that question: Never.

A kiss was a just start.

He supported her back as he glided his hands over her breasts, teasing the dusky nipple between his fingertips and cupping the fullness. The smoothness of her flesh enticed him; she was too silky to be real. She made small, feral noises in her throat as he prolonged their kiss.

"Yikes." She jumped and looked down.

Fat, orange Taffy meowed and rubbed against Jayne's legs again. A small black-and-tan goat poked his nose through the door.

"Jealous?" Jayne asked.

"Are you asking me or the cat?"

"Show me the second bedroom."

He led the way down a short corridor that went to the bathroom. He removed a small, framed photo on the wall beside the door to the rear bedroom. Revealed behind the photo was a keypad. He felt sheepish about his secret keypad lock. An escape from sensory overload was an adult explanation for this extreme solitude. The locked bedroom seemed more like a teenager's secret hideout.

He punched the code into the pad, waited for the click, twisted the handle and opened the door for her.

If his life had been a movie, this was the time for dramatic chords to swell. Jayne was entering his world. There was much about her that he liked. She had natural charm and sensuality. When it came to intelligence, she ranked among the smartest people he'd ever known. He liked her decisiveness, her wit, her strength and her kindness toward her patients. In many ways, she seemed to be the perfect woman for him.

They were a good fit when it came to sex, too. If their kisses and brief caresses were a preview of coming attractions, he couldn't wait for the feature presentation.

She sauntered through the room, passing the long table at the front where an array of computers and electronics were scattered.

Technically, this was a bedroom because there was a single bed pushed up against the wall. But the rest of the large space was devoted to shelves in the closet that held equipment and supplies, more tables and a two-person gaming area where he tested his products.

She studied the photos on a bulletin board. "From the Mars rover," she said. "And a desert. And this looks like the bottom of the ocean."

"I was creating a habitat." He wished she'd turn around and look at him. It was hard to know what she was thinking when he was staring at her shoulder blades. "I design computer games."

She focused on a piece of equipment attached to the ceiling. "What's this?"

He pulled it down. "A periscope."

"You have a periscope in a mountain cabin?"

"So I can watch the flying lizards." He adjusted the scope so she could see through it. "Take a peek."

"If I actually see flying lizards with this," she warned, "I'm going to freak out."

When she put her eyes to the scope, he guided her fingers to the dials. "You can zoom in or out or make the image sharper with these."

She played with the focus and turned the scope in different directions. He stood behind her with his hands on her tiny waist. "What do you see?"

"Amazing perspective," she murmured. "The far-away cars on a distant road seem to be the same size as the leaves on a bush."

"I like watching the weather. I can almost see the wind."

When she stepped back from the scope, she noticed a

rectangular box on a table in the corner. "Oh, my God, Dylan, you have a 3-D printer."

Her excitement popped and sizzled like fireworks as she scampered across the floor to the machine and caressed it. She might have thought the periscope and drawings were somewhat interesting, but the 3-D printer lit a fire inside her. In a flash, she turned into a woman who could communicate with him on a creative level. He believed they could build perfect fantasies together.

Chapter Eleven

"I want brains," Jayne said, her voice fluttering with excitement. "I want to make models of brains. I've been dying to get my hands on a 3-D printer."

"We could do that," he said.

When she spun around and faced Dylan, she knew that she was grinning, because the bruise on her jaw hurt. She wasn't totally euphoric, but a stream of endorphins had lifted her mood. Building brains sounded like fun. And when was the last time she'd done something just for the fun of it?

"They could be transparent." She'd seen many varieties of brain models and modeling. Some showed the nerve endings. Others indicated blood flow. Others were artistic replicas of the swirling folds of the cerebrum and the chambered cerebellum. "I've got a lot of ideas."

"That's all you need."

"I can't wait." Playfully she grasped each of his arms and gave him a shake. "What have you done to me, Dylan?"

"Me?"

"It must be you. You're the one responsible for the way I'm feeling. I want to have fun."

"Everybody likes fun."

"Not me." Her grin became a chuckle. "And I never talk about my feelings."

Could there have been something else that caused her limbic system to blast into orbit? She considered the events of the past few days: an attack at her house, a strange meeting with her dad, a successful operation and an attempted abduction. The good outcome from Dr. Cameron's procedure was cause for celebration, of course, but she was goofy and giggly. "I'm a neurosurgeon, not the sort of person who gets excited about making models on a printing machine."

And, yet, she was giddy.

Taffy sashayed into the room, leaped onto a table by the door, struck a pose and glared at them. Maybe these animals had lightened her mood. Seeing a cat certainly wasn't uncommon, but the combination of cat, camel and ferrets might have affected her. She wondered if it was okay for the camel to be untended for this long. "Should we check on Loretta?"

"She's good. Even if she wanders off, the property is fenced." He made a square box with his fingers. "She's contained, like in here."

Contained? She looked at all four walls, noticing a great many photos and shelves and a sheet of water sliding down a flat slab of granite. "There are no windows in this room."

"It's supposed to keep the animals out and the dust down," he said. "Plus the ambient light is good for staring at screens for hours."

"And you've got the periscope," she teased, "which seems appropriate for a secret hideout."

He winced. "You picked up on that vibe, huh?"

"I did."

"You're not buying my mature 'sensory overload' bit?"

"Oh, I believe that, too. You're complex and interesting, but you're also a guy who likes his toys. Men enjoy playing with gadgetry and vehicles."

"What about women?" he asked. "What about you?"

"I like grown-up games." She walked her fingers up his chest and over his chin to his mouth. "I like games that involve lips."

"We're in agreement," he said. "Should we take this discussion to the other bedroom? It's more comfortable."

"Not yet. I want lunch."

A second cat—this one was white with black splotches or vice versa—joined Taffy on the table and whapped a computer screen with an all-black tail.

"Hey, you." Dylan picked up the cat. "Jayne, would you grab Taffy?"

"Why?"

"When the cats get in here, they mess up my equipment. That's why I usually keep this room locked."

She noticed two other cat faces in the doorway. "How many cats do you have?"

"Many."

She snuggled Taffy into her arms, and the cat climbed so his head was nestled under her chin. She could hear him purring against her collarbone as she strolled toward the door. Growing up, she'd never had pets. When her dad lived at the ranch in Texas, there'd been livestock but they were mostly for eating.

In the hallway outside his secret room, Dylan locked the door. Over his shoulder, he said, "I notified your father to let him know you're in a safe place. And I told Eloise to cancel your appointments for the rest of the week."

"Wednesday, Thursday, Friday, that's too long." She didn't like to take time off. Her schedule was tight. "I should go back by Friday."

"It's not up to me," he said. "As long as Koslov is on the loose, you need to stay here."

Her fleecy pink clouds of euphoria were showing their dark underbellies. She didn't want problems. She needed to have her happy mood back. "I can compromise. I'll work via phone conference and email."

"We'll figure out a way for you to stay in touch, but the timing will be limited. If you're connected to a phone signal, Koslov can trace the call and pinpoint your location."

"Is he tech savvy enough to do that?" she asked.

"He's not, but Tank Sherman is." Dylan unceremoniously dropped the black-and-white cat, which dashed across the floor and vaulted onto the windowsill. "Koslov used the kid before to breach your security system and might use him again to track your cell phone."

"How do we get around that?"

"Third party," Dylan said. "You call my brother at the TST Security offices, where the phones are encrypted and untraceable, and then Sean relays the message."

How could she possibly work that way? Passing messages from one person to the next sounded like an annoying children's game. There had to be an alternative.

She turned on her heel and went into her bedroom to change out of her pajamas. Jayne was pleased to find her clothing neatly tucked in dresser drawers and hanging in the closet.

If an emergency arose and she needed to get back to work, they'd have to find a way to get her back to the hospital, and ditto for her phone calls. Jayne was in charge here. She was footing the bill for a bodyguard, and his job was to make sure she didn't get attacked on his watch. He didn't get to make the rules about where she stayed and who she talked to.

Though it was September in the mountains, she'd been plenty warm enough in her pajamas. She threw on a pair of jeans, red-and-blue sneakers and a comfortably faded red hoodie over a white zip-up tank top. In the bathroom, she yanked up her hair and checked out the bruise on her face.

When she'd told Dylan she wasn't someone who went

chasing after fun and good times, she hadn't been lying. At one time, Jayne had thought she was the only person in her age bracket who didn't play online games. It wasn't a conscious choice—there just wasn't time when she was busy with her studies. *Pathetic?* Some people might think so.

Some people, like her father or one of the idiot women he married, would hover over her and demand that she partake in some sort of "fun" event. Because Dad had insisted, Jayne had gone to her senior prom, never mind that she was a thirteen-year-old senior in high school.

Outside on the porch, she felt the warmth of a Colorado blue-sky day beaming down on her. She stretched and rotated her shoulders, noticing a few aches and twinges from getting banged around in yesterday's escape. The flat of her hand rested on her belly. The last time she'd eaten was the tuna sandwich from Mrs. Cameron. "I'm starving."

"Betty always has something on the burner."

The breeze smelled fresh and clean even though she saw a plume of smoke from the sprawling, two-story cedar lodge beyond the forest and down an asphalt road. Much closer, at the foot of the cabin's porch stairs, Loretta sat without moving. Her long lashes were at half-mast, and she looked bored. A brown goat was curled up beside her with his head resting against her side.

"Who's Loretta's little friend?" she asked.

"That's Romeo. He has four fat nannies to frolic

around with, and he's in love with the camel." He approached Loretta. "Do you want to ride or should I?"

Though she wasn't sure this counted as fun, she'd never taken a ride on a camel before. "Is there a trick to it?"

"If you know how to ride a horse, you can do this. Loretta was trained to obey the same commands."

"I'll ride."

He shooed away the goat and took her hand as she approached the woolly Bactrian camel. "It's best to mount while she's sitting. Just climb onto the saddle between the humps and hang on. After she stands up, I'll adjust the stirrups."

Jayne mounted without any major problem. But when Loretta stood in a seesaw motion with back legs first, then the front, balance was an issue. She nearly slipped off into Dylan's arms. Scrambling and grabbing the humps and trying to hold on with her knees, she got herself upright in the saddle again.

After he shortened the stirrups, she took the reins in hand. "Okay, Loretta, let's move."

The camel shook her head from one side to the other, opened her mouth and made a flat, ugly noise.

Jayne leaned forward to pat Loretta's long neck. "It's okay, girl. Take your time. You can go whenever you want."

"Don't tell her that," he said. "This is a stubborn lady. She likes to stand around."

"She doesn't understand what we're saying," Jayne

said, chastising herself. *What's happening to me? Am I talking to a camel, really?* "Just go."

He took the harness and started walking Loretta along the road toward the house. Her gait was wobbly but the experience was not significantly more uncomfortable than riding on horseback. Jayne could get accustomed to travel by camel.

"Why is Loretta at RSQ?" she asked. "Is she ill?"

"The guy who owned her had a plan to raise camels, but he only could afford three, and it got too expensive to care for them."

"Why raise camels?"

"For the wool," he said, "like llamas. Also, camels give milk. Betty made cheese from Loretta's milk, and it wasn't horrible. I guess there are nomadic tribes who live on camel milk."

By any stretch of her imagination, this was a bizarre conversation. She looked down at his wide shoulders as he walked in front of her, leading Loretta. When she noticed the gun on his hip, she remembered that this visit to RSQ wasn't all about fun and games. This was a safe house. She was as much a victim as these animals, maybe even more so because she wasn't being neglected. Koslov was hunting Jayne.

"What will happen to Loretta?"

"A zoo in Montana took the other two camels. We'll find a spot for her."

Romeo the goat trotted along beside them. When the female goats got close, he actually lowered his head and took a run at them. "Romeo's mean," she said. "Where did the goats come from?"

"A petting zoo that went belly-up."

As they neared the house, an older woman with a long, silver braid rushed out the door. She gestured for them to hurry.

Dylan broke into a jog and so did Loretta. The two of them moved in a neat, synchronized motion. By contrast, Jayne jostled wildly between the humps. This saddle was a high seat. If she fell from here, it was going to hurt.

"Let me off," she said.

She swung her leg over the hump and slid down the saddle. Dylan caught her. Gently, he set her on the dirt beside the camel.

The silver-haired woman from the house jogged up close to them, dusted off her palms on her jeans and stuck out her hand. "I'm Betty Burton. Dylan tells me that you're a doctor."

"Yes," Jayne gasped.

"I don't suppose you've ever worked with animals."

Jayne introduced herself and returned the firm grip. "I haven't got vet experience, but maybe I can help. What's the problem?"

"Over there in the barn, we've got a giraffe going into labor."

Another first in Jayne's life. She hoped it would be the last time she played midwife to a giraffe.

Chapter Twelve

Dylan hustled Jayne toward the barn. Her neurosurgery skills wouldn't be much use with a pregnant giraffe, but she knew the basics of doctoring and blood didn't scare her.

When RSQ had agreed to take Bibi, short for Big Bertha, the interior of the barn had to be reconfigured. They'd kept the horse stalls along one wall. On the opposite wall, they'd shuffled some of the smaller pens and moved the goats outside to their own enclosure. In the center, at the apex of the barn, a large area was marked off with tall chain-link fences. That was where Bibi was kept. Her food was set out on the second story of the barn where the hay was stored in bales. All she needed to do was stretch her long neck and chomp. Outdoors would have been better, but she was just too big and too fast if she decided to make a run for it.

Betty's husband, Tom, greeted them at the double-wide barn doors with his cell phone in hand. He gladly passed it to Dylan. "It's the vet."

"Hey, Doc, I've got a woman here who's an MD. Her name is Jayne. Why don't you talk to her?"

He passed the cell phone to Jayne and asked Tom, "How do you know she's ready?"

"Same way as with a human. Her water broke." The old cowboy jabbed his thumb toward a messy corner of her indoor pen. "I wasn't sure what to do next. So I called the vet in Buena Vista."

"Will she get here in time for the birth?"

He shrugged and rubbed his hand along his clean-shaven jawline. "Beats me."

A man of few words, Tom Burton didn't demand much attention. Quietly and efficiently, he managed RSQ Ranch and took care of the animals. His wife handled the people part of the business. Dylan considered himself lucky to have hooked up with the Burtons.

While talking to the vet, Jayne was clearly in her element. She wrapped up the conversation with a promise to contact the vet after the birth. Calmly, she approached the pen. "This doesn't sound difficult at all."

"Most species of giraffe reproduce well in captivity," he said.

Dylan eased open the gate and stepped inside the pen with Jayne at his side. "Did the vet tell you anything we're supposed to do?"

"She said labor seldom lasts for more than a couple of hours and mostly consists of pacing and groaning. No trouble at all."

He didn't believe for one minute that delivering the

calf would be easy. The vet tended to oversimplify. "When the time comes, will Bibi lie down?"

"Not usually."

Jayne stood very still while Bibi lowered her long neck and brought their faces close together. Jayne reached up and stroked the giraffe's cheek. Gazing into each other's eyes, they seemed to have a sweet and empathetic connection. Dylan took his phone from his pocket and framed a picture of Jayne's dark curls and Bibi's white face with the dark spots on her neck. The charm didn't last for long. Bibi stuck out her long, dark purple tongue and coiled it around Jayne's wrist.

To her credit, Jayne didn't shriek. "Not expecting that," she said. "It's a little gross."

Bibi raised her head and returned to her pacing. He wished the pen was bigger, but the vet had told him it wasn't good for her to have too much room.

"Look!" Jayne pointed.

The scrawny calf's legs were sticking out. Bibi paused to lick around the edges and went back to her pacing.

"You didn't answer me," he said. "If she doesn't lie down to give birth, what does she do?"

"She spreads her back legs and gives a push and splat—the calf comes out." She illustrated by stretching her legs apart and gesturing. "These are big babies, over six feet tall and over a hundred and twenty pounds. The umbilical cord snaps when the calf falls, and the bump is enough to get breathing started. All in all, it's quite efficient. Bibi will groom her calf, and the little one should get up and walk within a few minutes."

He saw the legs hanging from Bibi's rear. It didn't look at all normal. "That's a long fall to the ground."

"And that's where you come in," she said brightly. "Someone needs to catch the baby. At least, break the fall."

Somehow, this had gone from "no problem" to him standing under the back end of a giraffe waiting to catch a 120-pound baby. He might have argued but doubted it would do any good. Dylan was the tallest and the biggest among them.

He heard Tom Burton chuckle and shot him a glare. "You think this is funny?"

"Indeed, I do, and I'm planning to take pictures."

He entered the chain-link enclosure with Bibi and glanced over at his audience. There was Jayne, of course, and Tom. And a collection of barn cats, ferrets and goats. Several lop-eared bunnies stood at the edge of their large pen wiggling their noses. The cats formed two groups. Four of them perched in a row on a hay bale watching Bibi. Several others nudged Tom and meowed for food.

Jayne reached down and petted a fluffy gray cat that purred as loudly as a motorboat and wouldn't stop rubbing against her legs.

"You're a pushy one," Jayne said. "And it won't do you any good to kiss up. I don't have food."

Dylan hooked his fingers in the chain link and stared at her. "Did I just hear you talking to that cat?"

"Oh, my God, I'm turning into one of those people."

"Kindhearted animal people," he said. "Card-carrying members of PETA."

"Okay, animal lover." She pointed to the giraffe. "Here comes the head."

The head and long neck joined the legs. A gooey-looking placenta peeled back from the baby's face. Dylan saw the eyelashes flutter as Bibi took a stance. It was time.

"Go," Jayne urged him.

"She seems to be doing a good job on her own."

"This isn't like the wild where she could find a soft spot to have her baby. The floor is a concrete slab. She needs you."

He moved into position and held out his arms. Bibi swatted at him with her tail, and he batted it away. He tried to squat under the giraffe's back legs.

When Bibi let out a moan and shifted her weight, the baby swung back and forth. More leg appeared. More neck. In a spurt, a long strange-looking creature slithered out.

Dylan managed to break the fall. He landed on the floor with a lapful of giraffe calf.

He scooted away from the calf. Bibi took over, licking her baby clean.

Breathing through his mouth, Dylan watched mama and calf. The gangly, adorable baby batted long eyelashes and nuzzled close to Bibi. Though he hadn't done anything but catch, he was proud of the role he'd played. How many Colorado cowboys could say they'd birthed a giraffe?

Chapter Thirteen

Urging her to hurry, Dylan led Jayne down the hallway in the big cedar house to an office with an L-shaped wooden desk that was part computer station and partly for writing. A row of black file cabinets lined the walls that weren't holding floor-to-ceiling shelves of well-worn books. The black plastic telephone on the desk looked like a piece of technology from years gone by that was being devoured by more modern equipment. He gestured toward the handset. "It's for you."

"My dad?"

He lowered his voice. "I called my brother at the TST office and you-know-who was there. He's insistent about talking to you."

Reluctantly, Jayne slid into the swivel chair behind the desk and picked up. "Hello, Dad."

"Where did you disappear to? I thought I was taking you back to Texas with me."

It was typical for him to make up a scenario that he hadn't discussed with her. She was utterly certain that she'd never given any indication that she'd return with him to Dallas. "I need to stay in Denver. It's where I work, where I live."

"I've had a chance to look at that little fixer-upper house you bought. It's not as much of a mess as I thought."

"Thanks, Dad." Her father didn't make concessions lightly. Every other time he'd referred to her house, it was the "dump" or the "hovel." Saying it wasn't a total mess counted as a compliment from him. Buttering her up? He must want something really bad.

"I could stay at the house with you until this is over," he said in a reasonable tone. "I could bring in some contractors and finish up some of the repair work."

As if they'd ever worked together on a project without being at each other's throats? He was dangling a carrot, and she wanted to know why. "What do you want, Dad?"

"Tell me where you are?"

"In the mountains."

"Where, exactly, in the mountains?"

She repeated a version of what Dylan had said about hideouts. "A safe house isn't very safe if other people know where it's located."

"At least, give me a phone number."

"I'm not sure how this works." She looked across the home office to Dylan, who was leaning against the doorjamb. "Can we put this call on speaker?"

He extended his long arm and pressed a button on

the computer attached to the phone. "Hello, sir. Can you hear me?"

"Loud and clear."

Her dad didn't sound happy about talking to Dylan, probably because he thought he could convince her to do what he wanted if no one else interfered. When was he going to learn that she made her own decisions and was stubborn as hell?

"Dylan," she said as she swiveled toward him, "can explain the telephone situation to you. Okay, Dad?"

"First I've got a bone to pick. Dylan, you gave me a burner phone and told me I could use it to contact you."

"Yes, sir," Dylan said. "And I'd appreciate if you keep that cell phone with you in case we need to make contact."

Her father's voice went loud. "Doesn't work, the damned cell phone doesn't work. The only place I can call is the TST Security office."

"Which is how you reached us this morning," Jayne pointed out. "Please continue, Dylan."

"As I'm sure you are aware," he said, "cell phone signals and technology are linked to GPS and can be tracked. Records for landlines are also accessible. If you had a phone number for Jayne and called it, anyone monitoring your phone could locate her."

"Of course, I know that. Everybody knows that."

"I've developed an ironclad firewall to protect the cyber-interconnections between the phone at the TST Security office—the one you're talking on—and my phone at the safe house. The signal bounces all around the globe before it's relayed. If a third party gets close, our words shred into binary code."

"Our government could use technology like that."

"Yes, sir, they already use it."

Her father's voice took on a huffy tone. "Are you saying that *our* government uses *your* technology?"

"I'd never be allowed to say that."

She studied him as he sat on the edge of the desk and delivered his explanation. Which variation of Dylan was this? He was dressed like a cowboy in jeans and a plaid cotton shirt with the sleeves rolled up. But his tone and his mannerisms seemed more like the professor. And his words were as confident as a business mogul and had resulted in a sly put-down of her dad, which Jayne, of course, cherished.

Her mind was still digesting the information she'd learned from Betty about Dylan being a child genius. His field of interest was far different from hers, and he'd already hinted that he didn't do well in school... maybe because his parents were schoolteachers? And she sensed the loneliness inside him, similar to her experiences.

"Jayne, what do you say?" her father asked. "Come back to Denver and we'll stay at your house. I'll hire more bodyguards. If Koslov dares to show his ugly face, we'll grab him."

Dylan shook his head. On a legal pad, he wrote, "Using you as bait."

Aloud, she said, "That sounds like you're setting a trap for Martin Viktor Koslov, and using me to lure him in."

"I'd never do anything to hurt my girl," he said.

"Excuse me." The smooth, lightly accented baritone of Javier Flores interrupted. "I would be honored if you both stayed with me until the danger had passed."

Dylan's head shaking became emphatic. In huge letters on the legal pad, he wrote, "NO!"

Flores continued, "I already have top-notch security and a full-time contingent of bodyguards."

"Why do you need so much protection?" she asked.

"My father made enemies when he established our family business. Even a legitimate entrepreneur such as myself runs into conflicts with the likes of Diego Romero. In the past, I have been targeted."

"What about your wife and kids?"

"Ex-wife," he corrected. "And I have not been blessed with children of my own."

The fact that he hadn't settled down and started the next generation of Flores offspring made her think he might be younger than she'd presumed. "I couldn't impose. The search for Koslov might take weeks, and it doesn't seem right for me to move into your house."

"I'd appreciate the opportunity to learn more about you," he said. "And you wouldn't be alone at my house. Your father would be a chaperone."

"It almost sounds like you're thinking of this as a date."

"And if I am…"

His hints drifted on waves of sensuality. Since her dad wasn't objecting, she figured that Dad approved of Flores as a suitor. Many times, he'd told her how he wished she'd find a man, settle down and do her doctoring part-time.

"I'll consider both offers," she said. "Today and tonight, I'm staying right where I am. I'll talk to you tomorrow. Goodbye, Señor Flores."

"Please," he said, "you must call me Javi."

Short for Javier, it was a very breathy name. "Very well, Javi, goodbye. Same to you, Dad."

"Before you leave the TST office," Dylan said, "it might be wise to set up a calling schedule. We'll make sure we're close to the phone at the right time."

As soon as the connection was severed, he came around the end of the desk and blocked her way so she was trapped in the swivel chair.

"Here's why," he said, "it's a bad idea to stay with Javi. He has enemies in Venezuela. He even mentioned Diego Romero who we know is connected to Koslov. Before you even consider the possibility of staying at his mansion full of bodyguards, who might be disloyal to Javi and working for Romero, let me do a full background check on him to make sure he's one of the good guys."

She recognized the rush of words and the nervous tension. "You're jealous."

"Of him?" He pulled a face. "I don't care one way

or another about Javi. I'm just doing my job, guarding your safety."

She stood behind the desk, reached out and pushed lightly against his chest. "I haven't decided what I'll be doing or where I'll be staying." She gave another little push, and he stepped back. "Rest assured that it will be my decision. I call the shots when it comes to my life."

She pushed again. This time he didn't move back. He caught her hand and held it. "I have something to ask of you."

His voice was low and compelling. When she looked up into his warm gray eyes, she felt warmer and somehow safer. "Go ahead, ask."

"Don't put yourself in danger." He squeezed her hand. "I never want to see you hurt again."

With the many distractions of RSQ and the birth of the giraffe calf, her ordeal had faded from her mind. It seemed like a very long time ago that she had been drugged and captured by Koslov. Her hand rose to touch the swollen bruise on her cheek—her injuries could have been so much worse.

Dylan was right to remind her. She wasn't here on vacation. This wasn't playtime.

She promised him, "I'll be careful."

AFTER HIS CALL to Detective Cisneros, Dylan decided to spend the rest of the day with Jayne, mostly outdoors because the crisp September weather was idyllic and shouldn't be wasted. He found an old pair of glasses to replace the contact lenses that had been lost when he was being the giraffe's midwife. He had more contacts, but he preferred the glasses. From the way Jayne looked at him, he could tell she liked the glasses, too.

Gauging how she felt about him wasn't easy. Most of the time, she seemed to lump him in with everybody else who had given her a hard time. Occasionally, he really made her laugh. Or growl like a tigress. Once or twice, he'd looked at her and felt the heat. There was chemistry between them, but how much? He wanted to take a little stroll down that path.

As her bodyguard, he knew it was unprofessional to make a move on the woman who hired him. It wasn't as though they were on a date. He didn't even know if she'd agree to go out with him, and she must have told him a hundred times that she was the one who called the shots. She was the boss, and he needed to get a grip.

After lunch, they rounded up a couple of horses from the corral and went for an easygoing walk. Following a narrow creek, they rode into the wide Arkansas River Valley.

Jayne leaned forward in her saddle and patted her chestnut horse. "Why would anyone want to get rid of this fine mare? She's got plenty of spark left in her."

"You've got a good eye," he said. "That pretty lady is an American quarter horse, only five years old, and she's partly trained for rodeo. Her family ran into financial problems and left three horses with us until they get back on their feet."

"I'm not sure that's a good idea. Are you letting these people take advantage of you?"

"That's not how I like to think about it. I'm just lending a nice family a hand. Someday, I might have to sell these ponies. But not right now. For now, RSQ is like their foster home."

At the base of the hill was a half acre of aspen trees with their round leaves turned bright yellow. He directed her along a path that led across the sloping hillside and into the forest. Their horses picked their way through the white trunks. With aspen leaves shimmering around her dark hair, Jayne looked like a golden goddess.

Back at the barn, they took care of their horses and then visited the enclosure to admire the calf. Wobbling around on its long legs, the six-foot-tall baby was adorable.

Tom Burton joined them. "The vet stopped by. She checked out Bibi and baby. Both are fine."

"Did you show her?" Dylan asked. "Did you show the photos you took on your phone?"

"She particularly liked the picture of you sprawled on your bottom." He chuckled under his breath. "You might have a future as an ob-gyn."

"Yeah, yeah, did you tell her the calf's name?"

"She liked that, too."

"What name?" Jayne asked. "What did you call her?"

"The giraffe calf is named in your honor."

"Jayne?" She wrinkled her nose. "It's an okay name for a person, but for a giraffe?"

He agreed, but he'd wanted to do something that would forever link her to the event of the baby's birth. "I used your last name. The baby is Shack, short for Shackleford, and reminiscent of a very tall former basketball star, Shaquille O'Neal."

"I like having a giraffe namesake. Thanks, Dylan." She went up on her toes and gave him a peck on the cheek—a completely unsexy kiss.

After petting Shack and Bibi, they left the barn and hiked up the rise to his hideaway cabin. He kept the door locked, and the furry reasons for barricading the door were sitting on the porch, positioning their long, feline bodies to get maximum sun exposure. As soon as he opened the door, the cats shoved their way inside, followed by three ferrets with perky eyes.

As soon as Jayne sat in a rocking chair near the fireplace, a white cat with black spots, named Checkers, was on her lap. Jayne glided her hand over the pristine fur. "How does she keep herself so clean?"

"Constant tongue bath." In another time and in a different circumstance, that phrase might have had a more satisfying implication. He stretched out on the heavy leather sofa. "I've been meaning to ask. You say that you don't care for animals, but when I was in your house in Denver, I saw stuffed animals. Three cats with white fur."

"Maybe I wanted a cat when I was a little girl. I

don't remember." While she talked, she continued to stroke Checkers. "I don't dislike animals. I just don't have time for pets."

He sensed a cover-up; there was more to that story than she was letting on, but he couldn't force her to trust him. And he had a bigger problem related to keeping her safe.

She was safe at RSQ Ranch. And she hadn't been grumbling about needing to rush back to town. He wanted to maintain the status quo, but Detective Cisneros had another idea.

Their best lead was the Tank Sherman. It was confirmed that Koslov had used Tank to bypass the alarm system at Jayne's house. Because Tank had dropped out of sight, it was likely that Koslov was after the hacker. These flimsy threads of logic were enough to make Cisneros believe that Tank had information that might lead to Koslov.

The problem was, Tank refused to meet with anyone but Dylan. An inconvenient demand but Dylan understood. Turning himself over to the authorities would probably land Tank in jail for a variety of cybercrimes and hacking. That was why he insisted on a face-to-face with Dylan.

But he couldn't leave Jayne here without a bodyguard while he had espressos with Tank. Would she be satisfied with his brother as a stand-in? Sean was better qualified to protect her. He had FBI training.

But would she agree to a change in plans? She liked to think she was running the show.

Dylan had considered giving Tank the directions to RSQ Ranch and having him come here. But he didn't want the hacker to know the location of his secret hide-out. If Tank settled in, he'd never leave.

Somehow, Dylan had to make contact.

Chapter Fourteen

She and Dylan shared an early dinner with the Burtons, who were a charming couple, well-traveled, interesting and smart. As they talked and laughed, Jayne found herself unwinding. Her joints loosened, and her tension eased. Instead of zapping signals from one nerve synapse to another, her body electricity went on low current.

It had been a long time since she'd talked to anyone who wasn't a professional contact, either a doctor or a patient. High stress was part of her life, and escape was nearly impossible when she didn't have many friends outside work and no regular boyfriend.

Her gaze lingered on Dylan. What would it be like to come home from work and find him waiting? As soon as that question popped into her head, she realized how different she was from the little girl her dad had raised. Peter the Great would tell her that it wasn't a man's job to sit home waiting for her. It was supposed to be the other way around.

She doubted that Dylan worried about any of those

old-fashioned gender stereotypes. He leaned forward, elbows on the dinner table, as he excitedly described a new fly reel he might buy for his next fishing trip. She didn't understand half of what he was saying, but his enthusiasm made her grin.

Pushing his glasses up on his nose, he turned to her and said, "You'd like fly fishing. It requires skill and finesse."

"Don't you just bait the hook and drop it in the water?"

"Bite your tongue, woman."

This led to an involved discussion of casting, complete with physical acting out. Then he went into the philosophical, psychological battle between man and trout. This version of Dylan was nerd-like in his blind excitement and professorial in his explanation. And where was the seductive cowboy? Fishing wasn't something she generally associated with sex, but she liked the way Dylan moved his hips when he pretended to be casting onto still waters.

Later, they hiked back to the cabin, followed by the three female goats and a border collie that seemed to think he was herding their little group. "It's still early," he said.

The sun had gone behind the mountains, but it wasn't yet dark. "It's the changing time of day, when the tools are put away and goblins come out to play."

"Poetry?"

"My nanny used to tell me that every night."

"That's a little creepy," he said. "Were you brought up in an abandoned insane asylum?"

"It gets worse. Nanny would make a scary face when she said 'goblins.' Not that I was scared. I tried to stay awake and catch the monsters lurking in the shadows. I never did."

"Until the night before last," he said.

"When Koslov broke into my house."

The goats had slowed their pace, and the black-and-white dog nudged their backsides and gave a low bark. Jayne shook her head, and the evening breeze combed through her long hair.

"Maybe your nanny was right," Dylan said. "There really are goblins."

"Only in your fantasy games. Real life is harder to score. In our first encounter, I would be counted as the winner. On the second attempt, Koslov came close to successfully abducting me."

"And I wish we had learned more from that."

"Such as?"

"More." Whatever information he'd gleaned in his conversations with Cisneros and Agent Woody, Dylan wasn't sharing with her. He looked down at her. "Are you tired?"

"Not at all."

"I could teach you how to play one of my cyber-fantasy games. The scoring is real clear. You might even like it."

"Not tonight." She was feeling relaxed and wanted

to enhance that mood. "I think I'll pamper myself. I never have time to follow a grooming schedule while I'm working. And your brother was thorough in packing things from my house."

"That's a surprise. Sean's kind of a slob."

"Well, he brought my organic shampoo and conditioner, a skin-rejuvenating formula for the bath and several other lotions and potions. He even picked up my aromatherapy candle."

Opening the cabin door proved difficult. The goats tromped up onto the porch as if expecting to be offered a nightcap. The Border collie knew this wasn't the right place for goats and started barking loudly to get them to move.

The cats weren't happy. Fangs bared. Backs went up. Claws came out.

When Dylan finally got the door open, he reached inside and turned on the porch light. The animal action froze. Then the very clever collie shoved one of the goats toward the stair. In a few seconds, all was back to normal.

Dylan held the door for her. "If you change your mind or want some company, I'll be in the computer room."

"Thanks."

She watched him saunter across the front room and disappear into his secret hideout. Computer games—no matter how brilliant and creative—weren't much of an enticement for her. If he'd suggested a different activity, something more sensual in nature, or if he'd pulled her into his arms and kissed her mouth, she would have been happy to stay up with him.

It was only half-past seven o'clock when she sank into the steaming hot bathtub. Her aromatherapy candle smelled like lavender, which was recommended for stress relief.

While she was soaking, she applied a facial masque to tighten her pores and tidied up her fingernails and cuticles. She never did manicures, didn't like the flash of an unusual color in the operating room. But she went wild with her feet and toenails. At the moment, her polish was intense purple.

Indulging herself was fun, but she'd get bored if she went through these rituals more frequently. Jayne enjoyed bright, pretty, feminine things—like her wild underwear and bras. But getting dressed from head to toe in fashion seemed like a lot of work when all she really needed was to toss on a pair of scrubs.

After drying and brushing her hair, she dressed in a soft, comfortable nightie. It was white cotton with delicate embroidered pink roses at the ballerina neckline, and her robe matched. She caught a glimpse of herself in the mirror over the dresser in her room. With her hair washed and brushed shiny and smooth and her virtuous white gown, she looked as innocent as a virgin. Underneath, she was wearing fire-engine-red panties with black lace. Not that anybody would know.

Jayne wished she could enjoy the best indulgence,

which was having someone else appreciate her tight pores and tell her she was beautiful as he caressed her shaved legs. She imagined the appreciative expression on Dylan's face when he looked at her sexy panties. Her tongue ran across her lips, remembering how he tasted. Her nose wiggled, recalling his musky, masculine scent.

If she gave him the slightest hint, he'd be all over her. And she had the feeling that another of Dylan's mysterious talents would emerge when his clothes came off. Would he be a good lover? Did she dare to find out?

Seducing him wouldn't be fair. But it wasn't as though she was making any sort of promise about a relationship. Dylan was a big boy. He could make his own decision.

Stretched out under the blankets, she wiggled to find a comfortable spot. The RSQ Ranch bedsheets weren't as luxurious as the linens at her house, but the fabric was crisp and clean. The top blanket was a quilt with mostly blues and greens that looked homemade and had an interlinking ring design.

She felt a thud near the foot of the bed. Though her bedroom door was mostly closed, she'd had to leave a space so Dylan would hear if she called out in the night. For the cats, the open door was an invitation to party time. There was another thud…and another…and the big gray cat with the loud purr marched up to the pillow and lay down facing her.

She watched him for a moment. As soon as she closed her eyes, the cat batted a wisp of hair off her cheek.

"Hey." She raised a finger to warn him. "It's after nine o'clock. Not too early to be in bed."

The cat doesn't care, she told herself, *because he's a cat and doesn't live by clocks. And doesn't know what I'm saying, anyway.*

Determined to sleep, she rolled onto her side and attempted to sink more deeply into her relaxation. *Meditation might work.* As she tried to clear her mind, she was distracted by the sound of a creaking floorboard. Just across the hall, Dylan must be moving around, maybe peering through his periscope. Instead of releasing tension, her muscles clenched.

Maybe a glass of merlot would help.

She swung her legs out of the bed and slipped her feet into her scuffed moccasins. Then she threw on her robe and went across the hall.

As soon as she entered, Dylan looked up from his computer screen. "I thought I heard you moving around."

"Same here."

Simultaneously, they knew what they'd heard. "Cats!"

He stepped out from behind his computer, picked up the orange cat with one hand and his beer with the other. "Can I get you a drink?"

"Merlot?" she asked.

"You're in luck. I've got some in the fridge."

When he left the room, she closed the door behind herself and followed him to the kitchen, where she perched on a chair by the table. Outside, she could hear the wind whipping the branches of pine trees, but this little cabin was warm and cozy and beginning to feel like home.

"You strike me as a beer drinker," she said. "But there's a bottle of red wine in the kitchen."

"It's there for you. I noticed what you drank and asked Betty to pick up a bottle when she stocked the cabin."

"Thanks."

"My pleasure." He opened the dark wine bottle with a corkscrew and poured a healthy dose into a stemmed wineglass. "Do you have a favorite brand?"

"I'm not a connoisseur," she readily admitted as she took a sip. "This tastes fine to me. A glass of wine at bedtime is a bit of a bad habit. Not that I do it every night."

He sat next to her and clinked his beer bottle with her wineglass. "Do you have insomnia?"

"Not really." Her occasional sleeplessness didn't rise to the level of a disorder. "When I'm especially worried, I have trouble falling to sleep. I first noticed it during my residency, when I'd been working double shifts on a rotation that included emergency medicine. I could never work in an ER."

"I understand."

"I was terrified about making a mistake and causing harm to a patient. I'd stagger home exhausted, fall into bed and be unable to sleep. Then I did something really stupid."

Her voice caught in her throat. She'd never confided this story to another person. She was too ashamed. Would he judge her?

She watched his reaction as she said, "I took drugs."

His gaze stayed level and calm. "Did it help?"

"At first, it did. I hooked up with another resident who had the same problem. We wrote prescriptions for each other for sleeping pills, and they were wonderful… a little *too* wonderful."

She remembered those first few nights of perfect sleep. In the morning, she'd leap from the bed, alert and ready to take on the challenges of the day. "At first, I woke up refreshed. Since I was getting such great sleep, I figured that I didn't need more than five hours. My friend, the other resident, found another drug that would wake us up."

Though she and her friend denied their addiction, the roller coaster ups and downs got out of hand. "It didn't take long for us to get into trouble. We were haggard, unable to concentrate, abusing the dosage on the pills. But we told ourselves that we needed to do this. One of the senior nurses figured out what we were doing and threatened to report us."

"You could have lost your career," he said.

"I was terrified. I quit cold turkey. A month later, I found a middle-ground solution with the occasional merlot before bed. Only one glass. It seems civilized."

"And you're a very civilized lady."

She took a sip of her merlot, enjoying the tangy flavor on her tongue and feeling just the tiniest bit intoxicated. "How did we get started on this topic? I'm sure you don't care to know about all my bad habits, not that an addiction to prescription pills can be brushed off as a habit."

"Could have been a serious issue," he said. "You were wise enough to know when to stop."

"I'm lucky. My brain chemistry isn't set for addiction."

A lazy smile touched his lips. As he slouched in the chair, his posture was the epitome of *casual*. He reached up and tucked a piece of his long hair behind his ear. "Do you believe that all our behavior is programmed into our brains?"

"A big question." People had started religions and ended cultures trying to find answers to questions like this. "I don't think we're programmed, but I know that certain behaviors are genetic, similar to physical illnesses."

"I lean the other way," he said. "I think behavior comes from balancing the extremes. It's a matter of personal choice, like Aristotle's golden mean."

She winced. "I wish you hadn't said that. Because now I'll have to prove you wrong, and I'll feel bad."

"You think you know all the answers?"

"Well, I know more than an ancient Greek who'd never seen a laser scalpel, much less an MRI."

He took a swig of beer and gestured for her to get started. "Bring it on, Jayne."

She launched into a long explanation of neurochemical reactions and how dopamine affected behavior. "In experiments, I've stimulated a certain part of the brain and watched the subject break into tears, literally."

"But we're people," he said, "not computers. There's a whole lot about us that can't be explained. Your taste of addictive behavior wasn't about neurochemistry."

"It doesn't exactly fit with your golden mean, either. Would you say that my merlot is a balance between being a pill popper and a teetotaler?"

"I'm guessing that most of your behavior is finding a balance between your work and the rest of your life. You started taking sleeping pills so you could function on the job, and you quit for the same reason. I don't think there's a single spot on the brain that pinpoints your ambition, devotion and love for your work."

She was floored. People very seldom bested her in a rational discussion. "Good guess, cowboy."

"Thanks."

She watched him over the rim of her wineglass and gave him a few seconds to revel in his victory. "Now it's my turn to do a minianalysis on you."

"Take your best shot."

"In the few days I've known you," she said, "you've switched identities several times. You've been a computer nerd, a macho bodyguard, a philanthropist and a cowboy."

"Don't forget giraffe midwife," he said.

"You, my friend, are easily distracted. The opposite extreme is intense concentration that borders on obsession. When a subject finally grabs your interest, you study it until you're an expert."

He nodded, conceding the point. With his thumb and

forefinger, he rubbed his jaw. He hadn't taken the time to shave this morning, and stubble covered his chin. "Right now," he said, "right this very minute, I have another problem of extremes. You could help me solve it."

"Go ahead."

He rose from the table and stretched his right fist in one direction. "Over here is my professionalism. You've hired me to do a job, and I intend to do it well."

"I should hope so."

"On the left—" he held his left fist in the opposite direction "—I'm drawn to you in an unprofessional way."

A shiver of awareness slithered down her spine. Jayne liked where this was going. She also stood. "Tell me more."

"Are you wearing those red panties under that pretty white gown?"

"I am." She took her last sip of merlot and set the glass on the table. "What do you want to do about it?"

"If I bring these two opposing forces together, they might explode."

He put his two fists together and popped them apart. With one hand, he held the back of her skull. The other arm reached around her waist and pulled her toward him.

They kissed.

Chapter Fifteen

Jayne surrendered herself entirely to their kiss. His attention was all consuming, urgent, demanding her full response. She knew this kiss was nothing more than a normal physical process, but there was no room in her mind for biology. Instead of cataloging her response in terms of glands and limbic systems and secretions of hormones, she abandoned logic. Her mind went blank, happily. And she was floating on soft, billowing clouds.

The gentle pressure of his lips became harder, his embrace grew more intense and his tongue probed. From the first moment they'd met, this attraction had been building. This moment was inevitable. Her ears rang with amazing harmonies. His lean, hard body molded to hers, and she felt tingles of pleasure leaping from synapse to synapse.

Before she had recovered the ability to think coherently, Dylan scooped her off her feet. Her arms wrapped around his neck, and she snuggled against his muscled chest as he carried her to the bedroom, lowered her onto her bed and slid under the blankets beside her.

Lit only by edges of moonlight around the window shades and the glow from the front room, the room was dark. She could barely see his face, though his lips were only inches away from hers. He reached to turn on the bedside lamp, and she stopped him.

"The lamp is too bright."

"But I want to see those red panties."

"There's a candle in the bathroom."

"Atmosphere," he said. "I like it."

His departure from the bedroom gave her a chance to catch her breath. She wanted sex with him. There was no question in her mind about that. But she didn't want either of them to be hurt. Somehow, she needed to hold back, to stay in control.

She felt behind her head for the pillow and got a fistful of cat, instead. A hiss and a swat and the cat settled back, exactly where it had been before. One thing she was learning about cats: They knew what they wanted and wouldn't quit until they got it.

Some people might say the same thing about her. She craned her neck. *Hurry, Dylan.* If he gave her too much time to consider, she might change her mind. And that would be a shame. Or would it?

Maybe she was making a mistake. Jayne wasn't sophisticated when it came to sex. She was a klutz. She'd read all the studies about neuro-stimulation and sexual fulfillment. She enjoyed sex and achieved orgasm about 50 percent of the time. But she didn't crave sex, didn't need it.

Deciding to surprise him, she slipped out of her robe and nightie. Under the covers, she wore her sexy red panties and nothing else. Turning to the left and the right, she tried to find a sexy pose.

He returned with three candles that he placed strategically around the room. All were in containers, presumably to protect from cat attacks since the felines explored each candle he lit. The flickering light warmed the knotty pine walls and gleamed on the brass bed frame.

In this rugged cabin, the ambience reminded her of the Old West, and Dylan looked the part of a rugged cowboy in his jeans and long-sleeved shirt and vest, not to mention the gun he wore on his hip. He sat on the edge of the bed and took off his boots.

Somewhere between the bathroom and the bedroom, he'd removed his glasses, and she wondered how well he could see without corrective frames. "Are you wearing your contacts?"

"No. Is there something you wanted me to see?"

In a deliberately slow, languorous movement, she peeled back the blankets. A horrible thought crept into her mind. *What if she looked silly?*

No need to wonder. He gasped, and he gaped. His gaze stuck on her panties, and she felt like a regular femme fatale seductress. The hunger in his eyes was worth the price of her fancy lingerie.

She purred, "Do you like them?"

With his index finger, he tilted her chin up. Then

he leaned down to taste her lips. In a low, husky voice, he whispered, "They're even better than I imagined."

He drew a line down the center of her body from the hollow of her throat to her sternum, passing between her breasts and ending below her belly button. It felt as though he was claiming her for his own, planting his flag.

His head lowered to the spot where his finger had stopped. He tugged at the lacy waistband of her panties with his teeth, and then he kissed lower. He spread her thighs.

Tremors of excitement shuddered through her as he fondled, licked and caressed. Her back arched. She clenched her fists on the sheets. Her toes curled. Through clenched teeth, she said, "Oh, my God, I knew you'd be good at this."

When he sat up on the bed, he left his hand resting at her crotch as though he couldn't bear to part with that precious part of her. "I'm just getting started, Jayne."

In a moment, he'd unbuttoned his shirt and taken it off. Not an ounce of flab, his chest and abs were taut and sculpted. His jeans followed.

They were equally naked. She had her silky red panties. He had black jersey briefs.

He pounced. Shifting gears from slow and sensual, Dylan upgraded his passion to forceful, possessive and wild. His large hands pinned her wrists over her head on the baby-blue sheets while he covered her with nibbles and kisses, alternating hard and soft, fast and slow.

Straddling her thighs, his arousal was pressed hard and hot against her, and she wanted him. She yanked her hands from his grasp, and her fingers skittered down his torso with occasional pauses to feel the taut muscles and sprinkle of springy brown hair, darker than his sun-streaked ponytail. Her thumbs hooked in his briefs, yanking them down. At the same time, she struggled with her panties. *Why wouldn't these bits of clothing come off?* She needed to have him inside her. *Why was she so clumsy?*

Dylan took charge, calmly undressing her and then slipping out of his briefs. He glided his hand along her torso. "You're beautiful, Jayne, strong and beautiful."

"You're not bad yourself, and I'm an expert. Doctors see a lot of naked bodies, and yours is fine." She swallowed with a gulp. *Why would she say such a thing?* "I mean, I'm not comparing you to a cadaver or an ill person. It's just that…"

"I understand."

She was glad when he covered her mouth with kisses, preventing her from making any other dopey comments. He held her close with their legs entwined. His fingers were doing wonderful, exciting things to the tight buds of her nipples, and the sensations rushing through her were electric. But she couldn't wait. Her patience was gone.

Rolling across the bed, she was on top of him. Her fingers tangled in his long hair, and she held him so he couldn't move his head while she kissed him hard.

"I want you," she growled.

"Condom in the drawer of the bedside table."

She lunged for the drawer, upsetting the orange cat in her rush to find the condom. And when she finally had it, she tore the package open with her teeth. One of the ferrets jumped up beside her, grabbed the package and dashed away. Condom police? In seconds, she had Dylan sheathed.

"That was fast," he said.

"I'm a doctor."

"Okay, Doc, what comes next?"

"Foreplay is over. I want you," she said. "Right now."

He didn't need a second invitation. His long legs tangled with hers. He separated her thighs and entered her, slowly at first and then faster and harder. At the moment when she thought she was about to explode, he'd pull almost all the way out and slowly start building the tension again.

It became a dance. She'd never felt so graceful in bed. They were meant to be together. They fit so perfectly.

Finally, he led her, floating and swirling, all the way to a killer climax. Her world shattered, and diamonds rained down from the skies. All her life, she'd scoffed at flowery, romantic descriptions of sex, but now she felt like every gushing word was true. She flopped onto her tummy and exhaled a giant sigh. "Best sex ever."

He laughed and smacked her bottom. "One for the record books."

She buried her face in the pillow. "I didn't mean to say that out loud."

Though her eyes were closed, she no longer wanted to go to sleep. Her sexual experience—limited as it was—had taught her that it took at least two or three attempts before she reached orgasm. She and Dylan had set the standard high, and she couldn't imagine how it could get better…but if it could, she wanted to try. *Was it possible to die from pleasure?* As a neurosurgeon, she didn't want to contemplate that possibility. There were far too many kinky scenarios.

He lifted the hair off the back of her neck and nibbled her earlobe. "More wine?"

"A half glass of wine and a full glass of water."

"Feeling a need to hydrate?" he asked.

"Always good after vigorous exercise."

Naked, Dylan had left the bed and walked to the bedroom door when he turned and looked back at her. The blankets were in total disarray. Still lying on her belly, she hadn't bothered to cover herself. The candlelight cast golden shadows on her creamy white torso and shoulders, which were a marked contrasts to her shining dark curls. Her slender waist flared at the hips into a fine, round ass.

He took a mental photograph of her on the bed. The caption would be: Best Sex Ever.

He hustled through the living room to the kitchen. The lights were still on. After he took the wine bottle from the fridge, a beer for himself and a couple of waters, he turned off the lights. He usually left the curtains and blinds open—there was no need to protect from the prying eyes of strangers. No one knew their precise location, except for his brother.

He and Sean were very different people. Sean was six years older than Dylan and was definitely the alpha dog at TST Security. When he had been with the FBI, Sean had not only followed the rules but trusted them. It had been a shock when he quit.

Sean hadn't approved of bringing Jayne up here. Actually, he'd favored turning her over to the FBI, which was something Dylan refused to do. The feds had to work within guidelines, as did Detective Cisneros. Dylan, as a private security specialist, had more leeway. If he could contact Tank Sherman—who seemed like their only real link to Koslov—Dylan wouldn't have to arrest the little hacker.

Every spare minute since they'd got here, he'd been on his computer, actually on several different machines, trying to locate Tank. Slipping and sliding through the disgusting filth on the dark web, he'd learned that Tank had left town. But he hadn't gone far. He'd thrown up a marker for Dylan.

"Wanna talk," it read. And then the visual signpost faded out on the computer screen. Dylan hadn't found it again.

Hell, yes, I want to talk. Frustrated, Dylan groped for a lead to finding Tank. The kid must have information that would help find Koslov or, better yet, figure out who Koslov was working for. Most likely, it was Diego Romero—the aging cartel leader reputed to be Koslov's father. But maybe not.

Back in the bedroom, he handed her the wineglass. She was sitting up on the bed with the pillows fluffed up behind her. She had the sheet pulled up to her armpits and a goofy grin plastered across her face, but she was still sexy.

She raised her glass in a toast. "Here's to you. You're the very best bodyguard I've ever had."

He saluted her with his beer bottle and took a swig. "I don't think your dad would approve of my methods."

"Have you spoken to him?"

"Once this morning with you. And one more time before dinner."

Her dad also wanted him to come into town and set up a meeting with Tank Sherman. Peter the Great, working with Agent Woody, was prepared to offer Tank a good deal of cash if he'd betray Koslov. Dylan had tried to explain that money wouldn't do Tank any good if he was dead, but Peter wouldn't change his mind. Dylan might as well be shouting at a fence post. "He wants you back in Texas."

"Not interested, Dallas isn't my home."

"He wants to protect you." He shook his head. "I'm not sure why I'm trying to give you your father's viewpoint. I guess it's because I understand how he's feeling."

"Do you agree with him?"

"Like your dad, I think you need protection. But that's why you hired me."

"It's been a long time," she said, "since I was a baby bird being pushed out of the nest. I can take care of myself. Without any help from Dad."

From outside the house, the rhythms of the night shifted. The predator birds—hawks and owls—screeched as they swooped across the sky. The leaves rustled. The cats mewed. Horses stomped their feet and snorted. From the barn, the camel and two giraffes shifted in their stalls.

The atmosphere was different.

Someone was outside the cabin, walking fast, coming closer.

Chapter Sixteen

Dylan flicked the light switch and blew out the candles on the bedside table. Still naked, he picked up his gun, moved to the window and peeked through the blinds. A man strode up the gravel path to the cabin, not bothering to disguise his approach. He wore a black leather jacket.

"Sean," Dylan muttered.

"Your brother?"

"Maybe he's bringing good news."

"That's not how it works," Jayne said as she flailed across the bed, looking for her nightie and her wispy red panties. "Good news can always wait until morning. Bad news comes at night."

"What time is it, anyway?" He squinted at the clock.

"Almost eleven," she said. "Time for bad news."

Sean stomped up the stairs and across the porch to the door. He knocked hard and called out. No doubt he wanted to make sure they had time to get dressed if they were doing anything. For a moment, Dylan was tempted to leave his clothes off, just to irritate his brother. Not a good plan. Late-night bad news probably wasn't the best time to play games.

"Dylan," Sean yelled. "Open up."

He unlocked the front door for his brother. Two cats dashed in. "What is it?"

"I need to talk to you, both of you." Sean marched through the cabin and into the kitchen. "Have you got any food up here?"

"Half a cherry pie in the fridge."

Dylan never left anything on the counter. If the cats didn't get it, the ferrets would. It was only a matter of time before the beasts found a way to open the refrigerator.

Jayne emerged from the bedroom. Her puffy lips and flushed cheeks made a clear statement. Tying her robe over her nightie, she looked like a woman who had recently exercised her passions.

Pushing a wing of hair off her face, she asked, "Is everything all right? My patient, Dr. Cameron, isn't having problems, is he?"

"I gave our office number to the hospital in case they need to contact you, and nobody has called."

"Is Koslov in custody?"

Sean shook his head. "Cisneros isn't making much headway. After that messed-up traffic jam in the hospital parking structure, the DPD kind of look like fools. On the other hand, there is progress being made by Agent Woody and the feds."

"Sounds like a band," Dylan said. "Here they are,

ladies and gents, welcome them to the stage, it's Agent Woody and the Feds."

Jayne gave a polite giggle. His brother didn't bother.

"Anyway," Sean said. "Woody got a computer contact from that Tank Sherman kid, informing him that Martin Viktor Koslov was looking for Jayne."

"Is that how he phrased it? Looking for me?" she asked. "Did he say why?"

"I don't think so," Sean said.

Dylan sensed something deeper buried underneath her question, something she knew. In the parking structure when Koslov had her in his grasp, they must have talked. "Did Koslov say something to you?"

"When?"

"In the parking structure." He hated to remind her of those harrowing moments.

"I don't remember. I was drugged out of my mind, and I'd been slapped hard." Her posture stiffened as she slid into her doctor persona. "The blow to my face was nowhere near memory centers and, therefore, wouldn't affect my ability to recall. But the drugs might be problematic."

"You're the expert on memory," he said. "What can we do to bring back your recollections of that time with Koslov?"

Her lips pinched together. He had the feeling that she didn't like being the subject of possible experimentation. Did she think he was going to saw off the top of her head and peek inside?

She cleared her throat. "I think he asked my medical opinion."

"That makes no sense," Sean said.

"I'm aware of that," she snapped.

"But it's consistent," Dylan said. "The first thing you said when I got you away from Koslov was, 'I am a doctor.'"

"Why would a kidnapper care?" Sean asked as he sliced a piece of cherry pie and slid it onto a paper plate.

"I don't know," she said.

She gave a little flounce as she sank into a chair at the round wooden table. Dylan saw ripe sensuality in every movement she made. If Sean hadn't been here, he'd tell her. He'd show her how beautiful she was. All he wanted was to be alone with her tonight, to be naked, snuggled under blankets in the bedroom.

He glared at his brother. "Why did you come here?"

"Because I'm sick of all these people calling and dropping by the office. They're driving me crazy."

"Tell them to get lost."

"I don't want to turn away potential business," Sean said. "I want this mess cleaned up."

Dylan repeated the words he'd heard Sean say dozens of time. "Even though it's not a bodyguard's job to solve the crime?"

"Even though," He took a fork from the drawer. "The only way to find Koslov is through the Sherman kid."

"I've lost track of him." He'd tried dozens of links and programs, searching for a sign or signature that looked like Tank Sherman's work. Nothing. "To tell you the truth, I'm glad he's off the grid. Tank's a kid, no match for Koslov."

Sean went into the fridge and took out the milk carton. "Want some?"

"A glass of milk goes with pie," Dylan said. "I want both."

"Me, too," Jayne piped up. "I suppose one of the people popping in and out of your office is my father."

"Him and his buddy Javier," Sean said. "I gave them a project to investigate this afternoon. Find Diego Romero."

Her blue eyes flashed. "I thought Romero was really old and never left Venezuela."

"Maybe." Sean poured three glasses of milk. "But if Romero wants something from your father, maybe your dad can negotiate his way out of the kidnapping and move straight to settlement, thereby ending the threat to you."

Dylan cut and served the pie. "You still haven't told me why you're here."

"Yeah, yeah, I want you to look at this."

Sean reached into the pocket of his leather jacket. He pulled out a scrap of paper and handed it to Dylan.

"Numbers," Dylan said as he took a seat at the table.

"Dots and dashes and more numbers," Sean said. "I got a call on our supersecure line. You didn't give that phone number to Tank, did you?"

"Definitely not."

"Well, he somehow got it. He wasn't on the phone. It was a female voice. She recited the numbers and dots twice, told me that you'd understand and hung up."

Without knowing the context of the numbers, it took him a moment to grasp what kind of message Tank was sending. "These are GPS coordinates."

"I guessed as much."

"If I'm not mistaken, this location isn't far from Buena Vista." Though certain that Tank didn't know how to find RSQ Ranch, Dylan might have let slip a mention of something in this area that alerted the kid. "And there's another code."

While they ate their pie and drank their milk, he stared at the markings on the paper and reviewed the code protocols he was familiar with. It was a long list; he'd plotted out a computer game using established codes and two spin-off games from the first one.

In deep concentration, Dylan was aware of his brother and Jayne talking and he tasted the pie and he felt one of the cats rubbing against his leg under the table. But he wasn't really present. In his mind, he was scanning an endless warehouse of information, rifling through files, digging for the information that would fit Tank's code.

"Got it!"

He slapped the flat of his hand on the table so hard that the cat at his feet leaped up, bonked its head on the table, screeched and ran away.

Sean jumped back in his chair. "And that's why you can't trust cats. They're always doing something freaky."

"That wasn't odd behavior." Jayne reached out and summoned the black-and-white cat named Checkers. As the cat curled up on her lap, Jayne explained. "A startle response is an acceptable way of protecting oneself. You might react the same way to the sound of gunfire."

Before they got into an argument, Dylan stood. "Would you like to hear what the code says?"

They both gave him their attention. Since they really didn't care about how the code was used, he didn't bother explaining his process. "The GPS is going to take us into Buena Vista, somewhere near the Arkansas River. The words that I could translate are 'Key-Yak-Two.'"

Sean shook his head. "What the...?"

"I'm guessing there's a kayak shop. And Tank is hiding on the second floor."

"Question," Sean said. "Why would Tank come so close to RSQ Ranch if he doesn't know it's here?"

"I might have mentioned Buena Vista a couple of times, which would cause him to zoom in on the area." The hacker kid would love to find the hideout where Dylan created his software. "Oh yeah, and I used photos of the Collegiate Peaks—Mount Princeton and Mount Yale—for the background in a game."

Still holding the cat, Jayne bounced to her feet. "It sounds like you found him. Let's go."

"Whoa, there," Sean said. "You're not going anywhere."

Her jaw stuck out. "I most certainly am."

Dylan weighed the alternatives. If she stayed here, she was unguarded. If she went with them, there could be danger. But she had both Sean and himself to keep her safe.

Jayne and Sean batted the question back and forth until she firmly announced, "I refuse to stay here by myself."

Sean looked at Dylan. "A little help, please."

"I'm on her side," he said. "All in all, I think she's safer with us than alone."

"Thank you, Dylan." She pivoted and went into the bedroom. "I'll be changed in a minute."

As soon as she left the room, Sean punched his shoulder. "That's for taking her side over mine."

"You know I'm right." Dylan liked to imagine that RSQ Ranch was completely invisible, but that wasn't exactly true. With recent advances in surveillance technology, nowhere was truly safe. Too easily, Koslov could locate this place. And Jayne would be at his mercy.

"We could be walking into an ambush," Sean said. "You and I can usually kick ass, but we're talking about an assassin from the Romero drug cartel."

"Not looking for a fight," Dylan said. "We approach with caution. At the first sign of trouble, we call for backup. The local sheriff's name is Swanson. We'll alert him before we get there."

Dylan went to the front closet, unlocked a hidden panel and took out a green army duffel bag loaded with guns and ammo. Since buying RSQ, he'd given up hunting. It didn't seem right to be rescuing camels and chasing down elk. But he'd kept his rifles and miscellaneous firepower.

Sean raised an eyebrow. "That's a hell of a defense."

"Just being prepared. We'll take two vehicles."

Sean reached into a pocket. "Earbuds so we can communicate."

"I'll get a pair for Jayne."

He strode across the floor and went into his bedroom/ workroom where a couple of screens were devoted to his efforts to locate Tank. On one screen, a driver's license photo of Tank was displayed. His face was narrow. Though mostly clean shaven, his pointy chin sprouted a pathetic attempt at a goatee.

Jayne came into the room. "That's Tank? He looks like a teenager."

"He's twenty-six, only two years younger than me."

"And can barely sprout a beard—he's just a kid." She went up on tiptoe and whispered in his ear. "You're definitely a full-grown man."

"Do me a favor," he whispered back.

"Anything."

"Don't let my brother hear you say that. He'll never let me forget it."

She grinned and stepped back. "I won't embarrass you."

Her nearness fired enough electricity to power the whole valley and beyond. He wished they hadn't been so abruptly interrupted after sex. There was so much more he wanted to give her and to take from her.

Chapter Seventeen

The physical awareness of fear, including the adrenaline surge, tightness of breath, tense muscles and urge to scream, became more and more familiar to Jayne. As she sat in the passenger seat of Dylan's SUV, she felt a tic at the corner of her eye. That was new. The cherry pie she'd just eaten did a tango in her belly.

If they ran into an assault from the bad guys, there was nothing she could do to stop them. She didn't know how to shoot and had virtually no skills in hand-to-hand combat. A knife was actually the best weapon for her—she knew the location of important arteries and could slash them in an instant. Or could she? In her Hippocratic Oath, she'd promised not to hurt other people, and she couldn't imagine committing murder, even in self-defense.

But when Dylan had wanted to go after Tank, she couldn't stay behind and wait for him. She had to be at his side. She inhaled and exhaled slowly, determined to stay calm.

In Dylan's SUV, they drove from the shelter of the

narrow canyon where RSQ Ranch was located. The first time they'd been on this road, Jayne had been sleeping hard, recovering from the drugs, so the surroundings were new to her. She tried not to focus on the shadows where scary things could be lurking. When the headlights emerged from the dark forest, they were on a high mesa above the Arkansas River Valley. Lit by moonlight, the vista was broad and open. No danger could be hiding here.

She hadn't been to the mountains all summer, and she marveled—as she always did—at the scope of towering rocks and thick forest. Above it all, a pale half-moon arced high in the star-spattered heavens. She concentrated on the beauty. *Forget the fear.* A vast swath of land spread below them in an untamed valley enclosed by rugged hills. Since it was the middle of the night, there were few house lights.

"I should come to the mountains more often," she said.

"Now you have a reason," he said.

"What do you mean?"

"You're not the type of person who takes an aimless trip to the mountains. You need a destination. That can be RSQ."

"Would I be your guest?"

"You'd be my guest in my cabin…" His voice took on a husky, seductive tone. "You'd stay in my bed."

"I'd like that."

"I can't promise we'd be naming giraffe babies after

you every time you showed, but there's usually something interesting going on. You're welcome to visit when I'm not here, too. There's plenty of room. And Betty can do with the company. She likes you."

"I like her, too." Her gaze focused on him. His profile, illuminated by the dashboard lights, was strong but not perfect. His nose had a crook that meant it had probably been broken and badly reset. His jaw was too square, but his laid-back smile kept his features from appearing sharp.

Generally, she preferred men who were neatly dressed and groomed, but there was something about Dylan's scruffy appearance that made her want to tear his clothes off. Naked, he was amazing. As she thought of Dylan lying in bed, her fears began to fade away. Dylan the porn star? Another identity?

He was good at disguises but had always been straightforward with her. He had a face she could trust, and that was saying a lot. His brother, Sean? Not so much.

Dylan glanced toward her. "Are you putting me under a microscope?"

"Why would I do that?"

"A brain experiment?" His shoulders rose and fell in a shrug. "I don't know why, but you were staring."

"I wanted to make a tangible memory of you, a mental picture I could summon whenever I want to see you."

"Or you could call me."

"Sure."

That was what he said right now, but she knew better than to count on a "call me." More likely, when this was over, they'd go back to Denver, live their separate lives and never see each other again.

"You don't believe we'll stay in touch," he said. "You think you're going to have the best sex ever, then turn your back and walk away."

Was he a mind reader? "Were you thinking the same thing?"

"Hell, no."

"Are we bickering?" she asked.

"Maybe. I don't know."

Bickering was better than sitting there like a frozen lump of fear. "I think we are."

She figured that he was familiar with this winding road because he was driving fast. He went faster. His fingers tensed on the steering wheel.

"I'll keep it simple." He pushed his glasses up on his nose. "I like you, Jayne. We have a lot in common. You're smart and fun to be around. Among a hundred other positive attributes, you're great in bed. No way am I turning my back on you."

That was what he said now while his memory was still fresh. Only a short while ago, they'd been in bed together. The scent of their passion still clung to her nostrils. She could still taste him on her lips. Would he remember her next week? In a year, would he even recall her name?

She tried to explain. "I'm not dumping you or anything like that. But there's a good chance that we'll say goodbye when I don't need a bodyguard. It's just the way things are. We both have busy lives and no time for a relationship."

"Instead of starting with the rejection you seem to think is inevitable, start with something good. You like me. I know you do."

"No lack of ego on your part." She was teasing, but she appreciated his confidence. The way she felt about neurosurgery was much the same. She loved her work and knew she was brilliant. "You've probably had success with women."

"Not great success."

She found that hard to believe. "Come on, Dylan. Tell the truth."

"I'm almost thirty and not married. Not a winning scorecard," he said. "My parents are getting real frustrated with me and Sean. He was married once, but she turned out to be a wildcat."

"Divorced?"

"A total reboot." He waved his hand as though wiping an invisible blackboard. "Forget I said that. Sean's love life isn't a good example. I just don't want you to think I'm looking for a bride. You probably hear enough from your dad about getting hitched."

"I made a deal with my dad a long time ago. He doesn't push me about my lack of a mate or spouse if I don't get mad at him about his many marriages." She couldn't stop herself from adding, "He had his one great love in this lifetime. That was my mom. He'll never find another like her."

He reached across the console and picked up her hand. The warmth of his skin felt delicious. He gave a squeeze. "That's why you forgive your dad for not understanding you and being demanding. He lost his soul mate and was badly hurt."

"Yes," she said quietly.

"The same applies to you. You lost your mother. That's a deep wound."

And she'd been to enough psychotherapists to hear dozens of theories about how that loss had affected her. Had she chosen a career in medicine because her mother was a biochemist? Was she trying to be a surrogate for her father? Did she run from relationships with men because she feared love?

"Complicated," she said as she mentally slammed the door on those painful theories.

"I prefer complexity. I could spend a long time trying to figure you out."

"You make it sound like that would be fun."

"It would be."

This conversation was taking an odd twist. They were talking about the future and the past all at once. On the plus side, she wasn't scared anymore. "Betty Burton told me that you spent a lot of time alone when you were a kid."

"I still do," he said. "And I'm going out on a limb and guessing that you were a loner kid, too."

"Making friends was hard while I was skipping from one grade to the next. I was always around people who were older. I dated guys who were older."

"That must have been a treat for your dad."

She cringed inside, acknowledging that on the occasions when her dad paid attention to what she was doing, he didn't approve. And, sometimes, his judgments were on-target.

When she'd been sixteen years old and preparing to graduate premed from Stanford, she'd thought that she was madly in love with a drama student in his senior year. He was twenty...and gorgeous...and the biggest narcissist she'd ever known. His ego was the size of the Dumbo balloon in the Thanksgiving parade, but all she saw was the glitter in his eyes, the blinding white glare of his teeth and the mahogany-tanned ridges of his six-pack abs.

She'd gone after him with laser-focused determination, studying fashion magazines as though they were medical texts. She'd colored her dark brown hair with sexy platinum streaks, learned how to do a "smoky eye" makeup and bought a bra that transformed her A-cups into plump, healthy C's.

In the back of his Lexus, she'd given him her virginity. The sex was pathetic, messy and totally unsatisfying, even though she'd studied sex, too. Deciding it must be her fault because he was so gorgeous, she'd tried again and again.

Finally, in an act of sheer desperation, she offered to

drop out of medical school and move to New York with him. That was when the best thing ever happened—he broke up with her.

"I didn't do well," she said, "with relationships when I was growing up. What about you?"

"I was a typical computer geek. I'd get buried in my calculations. Every spare minute, I was on my computer."

"Skinny?"

"No tan, no muscles, thick glasses."

"And lonely," she said.

"So true."

"That's the curse of being really smart. The other kids ostracized me and, to be quite honest, I didn't blame them. I was totally caught up in my studies."

"I was never sad," he said.

"Me neither. My isolation came because nobody else could understand what I was doing, and that stung. But I wasn't depressed."

"When did you find people who could understand you?"

"In med school," she said. "For the first time in my life, I wasn't always the smartest kid in the room."

"My wake-up came during my first year in high school when I had a monster growth spurt. I was still a nerd, but a very tall nerd that coaches wanted to get into sports. I liked the stats and symmetry of team games, but they weren't for me. I started biking and running. And I found that those exercises were a good way to shut out the rest of the world and think. I've done Ride The Rockies twice."

"The bicycle race out of Grand Junction? Isn't that four hundred miles or something?"

"The last time I did it, a couple of years ago, the route was 465 miles and 40,537 vertical feet."

"Well, that's one thing we don't have in common," she said. If he was looking for a riding partner, he needed to search elsewhere. "I've always been a klutz."

He gallantly said nothing, but she knew he'd noticed. Wherever she went, there were spills and stumbles. That was why their passion had been so incredible for her. Every kiss, every caress felt choreographed, completely right in every way.

He drove around the edges of Buena Vista, which were less quaint than the downtown area where there were several diners, lodges, motels and hotels. In the spring, there were lots of tourists. This area was renowned for white-water rafting. Along the Arkansas were several small businesses, all of them dark and seemingly deserted.

She pointed to a sign. "Kayaks. It's an A-frame. That means there are two stories."

"I see it," Dylan said.

Her fear came rushing back, but it wasn't overwhelming. She could handle it. "Why aren't we stopping?"

"Sean and I agreed that we should treat this approach as if there's danger. For all I know, Tank is working for

Koslov. Or the computer communications were sent by Koslov."

"Not the message with the code," she said. "Koslov isn't that clever. If he forced Tank to send it, Tank would have embedded something to warn you."

They went silent. Her ears rang with each beat of her pulse. Tension coiled her gut. He drove about a mile and made a right turn away from the river and into a lightly forested area where he parked and killed the lights. Sean drove in behind them. They got out of their cars and met in the middle.

The chill wind made her glad that she'd worn her dark green parka with the fake fur around the hood. Though there was no one in sight, they spoke in low voices.

"We'll drive closer in one of the cars," Sean said. "We park near the river. The noise from the rapids will cover our approach. I'll go first and tell you when to follow."

"Got it," Dylan said.

Sean popped the trunk on his car, took out bullet-proof vests and handed them around. "It's going to be big on you, Jayne. I don't have anything smaller."

She fastened the vest over her parka and clothes. Not only was it too big, but the stiff edges felt like she was packaged up inside an iron shoe box.

Dylan passed out the earbuds and told her, "This device is active and transmitting. Turn it on like this and off like that. Tuck it into your ear, and I can hear you

up to three hundred yards away. Don't say anything unless you sight danger. Stick with me."

None of the instructions sounded particularly difficult, and she hoped she wouldn't somehow make a mistake. Her adrenaline was already pumping. Her pulse
accelerated as she climbed into the back of Sean's car
with Dylan beside her. Both men were armed with semiautomatic rifles and handguns.

She asked, "Should I have a weapon?"

"No." They spoke with one voice. The sound of their
actual voices mixed with the voices inside the earbud,
and they sounded like four refusals instead of just two.

"What if," she said, "someone comes after me?"

"Stay close to me," Dylan said.

"And if you get injured?"

"I won't."

This moment was a test of just how much she trusted
him. They'd already gone through a trial by fire at the
hospital when Koslov had grabbed her and Dylan had
pursued without hesitation. This was different. Dylan
was literally risking his life to protect her.

Sean nudged his car along the edge of the road. The
headlights were off. He parked and disabled the overhead interior car light before they opened the door and
climbed out.

The rushing sound of the river masked the little
noises they made as they crept through the forest. Sean
went first. She followed him. And Dylan brought up
the rear.

Staying on a path that followed the shoreline, they went through the backyard of a private home that was far from the river and close to the road. Very few people occupied the land closest to the water. Nearly every spring, the runoff from the high mountains sloshed over the river's edge. Flooding was a real possibility.

They crept along a narrow dirt track past pines and rocks and shrubs. Inside her parka and bulletproof vest, she started to sweat. Though she'd stumbled a couple of times, she hadn't fallen flat on her face.

The flimsy A-frame had a sign suspended from the peak of the letter *A*—KAYAK. The rest of the space on the road side of the building had signage listing brand names for kayaks, as well as rates for lessons, rentals and purchases.

More significantly for them was a sign on the glass window in the door. Dylan pointed to it. Wi-Fi was available inside. The owner of the kayak shack might be cyberpals with Tank.

Sweat prickled under her armpits and along her hairline. She clustered in a tight threesome with the two brothers who seemed to communicate without words. Sean had peered inside through the filthy glass window in the door. He lowered his hand and tried the door handle. It turned easily.

When they entered, moving quietly but not silently, Sean went to the single winding flight of stairs near the front entrance. The lower floor was packed with displays of kayaks, associated equipment and clothes. A trophy was mounted on the back wall near the cash register.

She stuck like Velcro to Dylan as he crossed the display room to the counter. Behind the counter was a door. He opened it slowly. This room had no windows. He took a Maglite from his jacket pocket and turned it on. The bright beam crisscrossed the messy back office where invoices and unopened mail spewed across a desk that also had a neat stack of personal checks in the corner. Was this shack a front for something else? Or just an example of sloppy business practice?

She heard her name being called from upstairs and moved to respond.

Dylan caught her arm. "I go first."

"That was your brother's voice." Surely, he trusted Sean.

She heard Sean in her earbud. "Come quick, Jayne."

Together, she and Dylan raced to the staircase at the front of the shop. Dylan went first. At the top of the staircase, he aimed his Maglite beam at hazy forms of sofas and chairs and desks in the semidarkness of a slanted second floor with only one window.

Sean squatted on the floor over the heaving body of a scrawny, shirtless young man whose face was bloody. Spatters of blood marked his torso and arms. He gulped down air in violent gasps. Convulsions caused the jungle of tattoos on his arms and chest to writhe.

Panic gripped Jayne's gut. A drug overdose? Where was the blood coming from? She recoiled, feeling like a turtle shrinking back inside her bulletproof shell. It had been a long time since her training rotation in the emergency room. She wanted to run away, but that wasn't an option. *I am a doctor.*

She pushed Sean out of the way and knelt on the floor beside the young man whose body jerked convulsively.

Accurate diagnosis would be difficult. First, she treated the symptoms, clearing the area so he wouldn't hurt himself as he convulsed. "Can we turn on the light in here?"

Through the earbud, she heard Dylan and Sean discuss the dangers of turning on a light. Since there was only the one window, they decided it was okay. In the dim glow of a bare lightbulb near the center of the room, the second-floor apartment was dull and dingy, as though every surface was covered with a layer of dust. She dragged over a cushion from the beat-up sofa. "Dylan, bring me a blanket and a damp washcloth."

She checked the tattooed body, neck and face as best she could while he was shuddering and lashing out. There didn't appear to be any severe lacerations. Nothing like a gunshot or knife wound. Most of the blood seemed to come from his nose.

When Dylan returned with the blanket and cloth, she touched the forehead of the tattooed young man. He was feverish. "This is Tank, right?"

"Yes."

"Does he have a medical condition that you're aware of? Is he epileptic? Does he take drugs?"

"I don't know his medical history. We're not buddies, don't hang out together. If he does drugs, it's probably only pot."

"Then, we have a problem." Immediately, she corrected herself. "Another problem. I'm guessing that Tank is having an overdose from an amphetamine-based stimulant."

"And if he didn't take it himself, somebody gave it to him." Dylan caught on quickly. "Somebody else was here with him."

And it wasn't someone she wanted to meet.

Chapter Eighteen

Dylan knew just enough about drugs to understand that they weren't for him. He didn't think Tank was into the drug scene, but if he was, his drug of choice would be an amphetamine, an upper, speed.

He called to his brother, who had taken a position at the top of the staircase. "We got a problem."

"I heard," Sean said. "I've been in touch with Sheriff Swanson. His deputies are coming, and he's got an ambulance on the way."

"We're not far from the hospital in Buena Vista. They'll be here in a couple of minutes."

"I don't get it," Sean said. "If Koslov was here and gave your buddy Tank drugs, why did he leave? This A-frame is a neat setup for an ambush."

It didn't make sense. Koslov was famous for not leaving witnesses behind. Why had he given Tank drugs? Why hadn't he launched an ambush? Why were any of them still alive?

"He doesn't want us dead," Dylan said. "He wants

Jayne. And he wants her in good shape. He's not going to come after us."

"Well, in case he changes his mind and we get into a shoot-out, I want you down here with me by the staircase. It's the only access to the second floor."

Glancing over his shoulder, Dylan saw that Tank's seizure was slowing down. Jayne had turned him on his side and elevated his head and shoulders. Through the earbud, Dylan heard her talking to Tank, asking his name, asking if he knew where he was.

"Is he saying anything?" Dylan asked.

"He's unresponsive," she said. "I hope the ambulance gets here before he crashes."

"Stay with him."

Dylan had the strong feeling that the only reason Tank was still alive was to pass on a message. Koslov had used the hacker as bait to lure them to this place, and his ploy had been successful. They were here. Why didn't Koslov attack?

It would have been simple for a sharpshooter to lie in wait, to kill Sean and Dylan and to grab Jayne. While Dylan listened to his brother talking to the 911 dispatcher and explaining that there was a potential danger in approaching the kayak shack, he rolled the scenario around in his mind. Why did Koslov hold back?

For one thing, Koslov didn't know who would show up at the shack. If Dylan had more time and had been more plugged in to the investigation in Denver, he might have sent Cisneros and kept Jayne safely tucked away at RSQ. Koslov wouldn't make an assault on a bunch of cops for no reason. He wanted Jayne.

And he didn't want her injured. That had to be the reason he hadn't opened fire when he and Sean had shown up with the prize Koslov had been seeking. He couldn't risk taking a shot at them and hurting Jayne. Why was it so important to keep from harming her?

Drug cartels weren't usually so considerate of the people they kidnapped. If they weren't deliberately cruel, they treated their captives with calculated disregard for their comfort. No food. No water. Captives would be held in wretched surroundings. He hated to imagine what would happen to a woman as beautiful as Jayne if her care and safety was left to the discretion of Koslov and his men.

Through the earbud, he heard Jayne soothing Tank as he tried to speak.

"Doc...tor. Jayne. Help. Me. Doc...tor."

"That's right," she murmured. "I'm Jayne, and I'm a doctor. And you need to relax as much as you can."

"Water," he said.

"The ambulance is going to be here in a moment. You can have water then."

Dylan gazed back toward them. Jayne stroked Tank's forehead with the damp washcloth, cooling his fever. At the same time, she had him wrapped in a blanket. He wasn't going to question her methods, but he wondered if she'd spent too much time poking at brains to remember basic first aid.

"You're shivering," she said. "Are you cold?"

"Cold, Doctor, cold."

Dylan heard the wail of the ambulance and wondered if Koslov was hearing it, too. The assassin wouldn't attack the local sheriff or the ambulance staff. There was no point, and shooting an officer would bring down the full force of Colorado law enforcement upon them. So much speculation—Dylan wished he had more answers.

When Sean went downstairs to let the crew into the building, he moved to the center of the room and leaned over Jayne. "He hasn't said anything."

"He's cold and wants some water." She looked up at him. "Since the ambulance was close, I didn't want to give him anything to drink that his body might reject."

"You mean, he'd puke."

"Yes. I have no idea what kind of drug is invading his system. I looked around here and searched his pockets, couldn't find anything."

"Koslov drugged him," Dylan said.

"Like he did with me."

"You guessed it." He tucked the edge of the blanket around the shivering form of Tank Sherman. "Why are you dabbing his forehead to cool him down and covering him at the same time?"

"The blanket is for shock. The washcloth is for fever. Patience is the main caregiving procedure now. Until they know what he overdosed on, treatment is problematic. I don't want to make things worse for him."

When it came to medicine, she knew what she was doing. His job was to keep her safe.

JAYNE RODE IN the back of the ambulance with Tank and Dylan. It was too crowded, but she felt responsible for the skinny, tattooed hacker, and Dylan refused to leave her side. She couldn't fault his behavior—staying with her was what a bodyguard was supposed to do. And she'd miss him if he left. To be totally honest, she felt very comfortable around the macho version of Dylan, probably because there was still a lot of nerd in him. With one hand, he held a semiautomatic pistol. With the other, he pushed his glasses up on his nose.

At the Buena Vista hospital, she conferred with the other docs, scrubbed up and joined them in the OR where Tank was on an IV and a breathing apparatus. The drug he'd been given had damaged his heart. Immediate bypass surgery was required.

Her greatest concern was, of course, his brain. Even a moment without blood circulation to the brain could cause irreparable damage. In the operating room, she observed with her gloved hands clenched behind her back so she wouldn't be tempted to interfere while Tank was hooked up to the cerebral-function monitor, a device to measure brain electricity. The neurologist at this small hospital was competent, someone she'd worked with before.

Through the observation window for the OR, she watched Dylan standing guard and remembered the last time they were in a hospital. Dylan wasn't moving. Sean came over to talk to him, and they stood with their heads together, no doubt discussing where her next safe house would be.

She wished they could go back to RSQ Ranch. As soon as that thought occurred, she recognized the irony. Her interest in the animal kingdom was minimal. As a child, she'd never really had a pet and wasn't interested in animals. But she would miss seeing the baby giraffe grow and riding Loretta the camel. There were horses in the RSQ corral that she hadn't met. And her fingers were itching to stroke the soft fur of Checkers the cat.

But that hideout was no longer a secret. Dylan knew the sheriff and his deputies, and they'd put together that he was both the owner of the RSQ Ranch and a bodyguard. If they returned, they might be bringing trouble with them, and she couldn't bear the thought that any of the animals might be hurt because of her.

She'd go wherever Dylan told her to go because she needed him to keep her safe. There were a hundred other reasons she wanted to be with him, starting with a desire to feel his lips pressed against hers.

The neurologist stepped up beside her in the OR and asked, "Is there anything we should be doing for this young man? In terms of his neural functions?"

"Not until after he's stabilized," she said quietly. "I'm sure there will be swelling of the brain and probably concussion. Before we loaded him in the ambulance, he was having a seizure, banging his head on the floor."

"Can I contact you later?"

"Certainly," she said. She didn't approve of Tank's lifestyle, using his intelligence to work on the outer fringes of what was legal and what wasn't. But she would never deny her expertise to anyone who needed help.

Since there was nothing she could do in the OR, she glanced toward the window where Dylan stood watching her. Though he wasn't carrying a weapon, he radiated protective strength and courage. If anybody got too close to her, her man would attack.

She patted the arm of the neurologist. "It was nice to meet you, Doctor."

"Same to you," he said. "Did you get the message?"

"What message?"

"The Sherman kid mumbled it several times, said the word message repeatedly. It was something about doctors and Martin."

Every other thought was wiped from her brain. She had a clean slate. She grasped his arm, "Come with me."

"If I take off my gown and mask, I'll have to scrub again and put on new stuff to go back into the OR."

As she pulled him into the hallway, she didn't care how many times he had to change clothes. She yanked down her own mask, then his. "This is very important. Tell me exactly what Sherman said, word for word."

"He repeated several variations on 'Dr. Jayne. Message. Jayne is a doctor.'"

She remembered when Koslov was holding her at the

parking structure in the medical complex. His words were unclear, but she'd told him that as a doctor, she was obligated to come to the aid of anyone who needed her help. She would turn no one away.

Still clinging to his arm, she stared into the eyes of the neurologist. "What else did he say? Tell me as much as you can recall."

Dylan had come up behind her. "What is it, Jayne? What's wrong?"

"Hush," she said to him, keeping her focus on the neurologist. "Go on, Doctor, please."

"Help Martin. Martin needs you." He gestured helplessly. "And there was another name. Diego. That was it. Diego needs your help."

She released her grip on his arm and stepped backward until she was leaning against the wall. "Thank you."

Everything made sense to her now. She closed her eyes and inhaled a deep breath. From the very start when he'd broken into her house, Koslov had made it clear that he didn't want to hurt her. No matter what happened, she would not be harmed.

He needed her skill as a doctor. He wanted her to operate on his father, Diego Romero, an elderly man who had probably had a stroke.

She looked up at Dylan and said, "This was never about a kidnapping. It wasn't about my father. Martin Koslov was coming after me."

Chapter Nineteen

Dylan couldn't believe they'd been so blind. And he wasn't the only one. The professionals, like Cisneros and Agent Woody, had wasted their time tracking down connections to her rich, powerful father. They were so sure that it was a case of kidnapping, and they were so dead wrong.

"Can we get a diagnosis for Diego Romero?" he asked."

"We need proof that he's incapacitated."

"His doctor won't say anything."

"Why not?"

"I wouldn't," she said. "Information about patients is privileged. Plus, Romero is a powerful man, the leader of a cartel. If he was weakened, he wouldn't want his enemies to know."

Her reasoning was on track. If the old man was suffering the aftereffects of a stroke and had lost his memory, criminals from other cartels would take advantage. Not to mention, law enforcement moving in. The Romero organization would be picked apart.

Why did Martin Viktor Koslov want Jayne to bring back Romero's memory? Secrets, the old man had secrets. He'd run the cartel for over thirty years, knew who could be trusted and where the stash was hidden. Koslov—who was probably the old man's bastard son— might see these secrets as his inheritance. He needed Jayne and her groundbreaking neurosurgery to open Romero's memory.

He wrapped an arm around her shoulder. "You're safe now."

"How do you figure?"

"We get word to Koslov that you refuse to operate." He guided her through a set of double doors and down a corridor. "He won't have any reason to come after you."

"Who says I refuse to operate?"

"Believe me, Jayne. You don't want to help this man. He's violent, cruel, evil, altogether a bad guy." He started walking her down the corridor. "Nothing good can come from operating on the old man."

"Where are we going?"

He hadn't really come up with his next plan. Returning to the shelter didn't seem wise. Koslov might be clever enough to follow them. The thought of a cartel assassin at large in his gentle sanctuary horrified Dylan.

He and Sean had talked about returning to the hotel in Denver, but he wanted to stay close, to find out if there was anything more he could do for Tank. Dylan knew it wasn't his fault that Tank had gotten himself hooked up with Koslov, but he still felt responsible. In terms of chronological age, Tank was an adult. But he acted like a kid.

He glanced over at the beautiful woman who strode down the hallway beside him. "I need to take you somewhere safe."

"Too bad we can't stay here," she said with a grin. "I mean, the place is full of beds."

"Was that a joke? Are you being funny?"

"Giving it a shot."

He considered it a good sign that she was able to smile after all the threats to her. Discovering Koslov's true agenda was sort of a relief.

He came to a quick halt and pulled her close. Her pliant, slender body molded against his. Through the layers of shirts and jackets, he felt her firm breasts crush against his chest. His hand slid down the curve of her back.

His lips joined with hers for a hard, hot kiss. Her natural fragrance mingled with the leftover smell of the river outside the kayak shack and the hospital and the metallic scent of blood. Life experiences crowded around them and deepened their connection.

Jayne was more to him than a client or a woman who needed his help. She was becoming central to his life, and he wanted her always beside him. She balanced him. If she weren't here, he'd go spinning wildly of control.

The double doors behind them whooshed open. A

loud, angry voice demanded, "What the hell are you doing, Jayne?"

Her father. Well, of course. Dylan separated himself from her. They'd been so tightly joined that pulling apart felt like tearing Velcro.

"Hi, Dad," she said. "And you, too, Javi. Would you like to hear what we've figured out?"

"Let me go first," said Peter the Great. "Dylan Timmons, you're fired."

"You can't do that," she said. "He works for me, not you."

"I'm not firing him because of this." He gestured toward the two of them standing close. "I get it. You're an attractive young woman, and men have a hard time keeping their hands off you."

She drew herself up. Her posture was ramrod straight. "Thanks, Dad, for the charming description."

Peter the Great was not cowed by her sarcasm. He thrust out his barrel chest. His resonant voice dropped an octave; he sounded like Darth Vader without the wheezing. "Dylan and his brother, Sean, took you into a dangerous situation. It was an irresponsible act. You could have been killed."

"I was never in danger," she said coolly. "We were able to rescue Sherman, and he had valuable information for the police."

"You can tell Agent Woodward when he gets here. After he takes a statement from Dylan and his brother, they will be dismissed. You will go with Woodward into protective custody, WitSec."

"Do you even care about solving this?" she demanded.

"I care about you." He jabbed the air between them with a forefinger. "I care about your safety."

"What about the truth? Do you care about the truth?"

"Of course, I do."

"Then listen to me," she said. "We all thought the attack by Koslov was about you. Peter the Great Shackleford is so important that a cartel sent an assassin to abduct his helpless daughter to make him change his mind about some kind of business dealing."

"And I'm sorry," he said. "How many times do you have to hear it, Jayne?"

"Never again." Her blue eyes went icy cold. "I never needed to hear it in the first place. Koslov was after a world-renowned neurosurgeon to operate on his father. He was after me."

Dylan heard a strange note of triumph in her statement. He doubted that she often got to tell her father that she was more prized and more important than he was. Being the target of a murderous Venezuelan cartel wasn't the sort of success to brag about, but it was something.

Agent Woody saved them from further awkwardness when he shoved through the doors. Another agent, also dressed in suit and necktie, accompanied him.

Both Jayne and her father went toward Woody. Both

were talking without pause. Both gestured dramatically as they stated their opinions about what should happen next. Neither hesitated in telling Special agent Woody exactly what the FBI needed to do.

The father-daughter resemblance was inescapable. The Shacklefords were a hard-driving family, and Dylan was pleased to see that Jayne was winning the battle for Woody's attention. The other agent was listening only to her and nodding like an FBI bobblehead.

When she mentioned Diego Romero's need for the neurosurgery that only she could provide, Dylan saw Woody's eyes light up. The agent held up his hand for silence. He spoke to Jayne. "Are you saying that Diego Romero is in the United States? That he's nearby?"

"I don't know," she said. "It's unlikely that a sick, old man like Romero would travel. It'd be easier to kidnap me and take me to Venezuela."

"If there's a chance that Romero is here," Woody said, "I need to take advantage of it. I need to coordinate with other agencies."

"Think about it," Dylan said. "Not only does he need Jayne to perform the surgery, but he also needs all that specialized equipment. You saw the operating theater. You know what it's like."

"What do you think, Doctor?" He turned back to Jayne. "Would most hospitals have the necessary equipment?"

"It's hard to say. MRIs and CT scanners are pretty much standard, but my work requires extremely delicate electro-imaging equipment. And how would Koslov gain access? I seriously doubt that a dangerous assassin can waltz into a hospital and commandeer an operating room."

"Right," her father said. "So, we can assume that Koslov plans to kidnap Jayne and take her to Venezuela where she can operate."

Peter the Great seemed proud of himself for drawing this conclusion. Dylan almost hated shooting it down. "Except for one thing."

"What's that?" her father turned on him.

"Koslov could have already purchased the equipment he needs. He could have created an operating room in a house or a hotel room or a clinic. Diego Romero could be there, under a nurse's care, waiting."

Peter Shackleford blustered, "How would he know what to get?"

"My work isn't secretive," Jayne explained. "I've done a lot to publicize my procedures. I want other neurosurgeons to adopt and improve upon my methods."

Her motives were simple and pure as opposed to the devilish complexities of Koslov and the Romero cartel. Jayne worked for the greater good. Sure, she was gratified when her skill and talent was recognized, but she hadn't become a neurosurgeon for the acclaim.

She didn't deserve to be stuck in the middle of this mess. She wasn't safe, and it was up to him to take her away from the hospital and get her to somewhere safe.

He hooked his arm through hers. "We're going now. My brother has a car by the emergency entrance."

"Sorry." Woody blocked their way. "I have more questions for all of you, including your brother."

"Jayne needs to be in a safe house."

"Agreed," Woody said. "This won't take long."

As Woody and his partner whisked Jayne down the hall and away from the rest of them, Dylan caught her gaze. He pointed to his ear where he wore the tiny, near invisible earbud. Did she still have hers?

She touched her ear and nodded. She'd be able to hear him.

Chapter Twenty

Though accompanied by the feds, Jayne managed to apologize to the staff at Buena Vista hospital half-a-dozen times for disrupting their ER, OR and admissions area. Sheriff Swanson and two of his deputies herded the various groups from one room to the next until Jayne and the two FBI agents were settled in the social worker's office in the admissions area.

A nameplate on the messy desk identified Grace McHenry, and Jayne had a feeling that Grace wasn't going to be happy about the way Agent Woody took over her office and scooped her papers out of the way.

"I don't think you should move those," she said.

"This is chaos. I have to move something." He turned on a small recorder, stated his name and hers and their location and the time. It was all very official, and she stayed on point as she described how they had learned about Tank and his whereabouts, then left their safe house.

"Where is it?" Woody asked. "I need a location on the safe house."

"I don't feel right about telling you." She didn't want Woody and the feds charging through RSQ Ranch, disturbing the cats, goats and camels. "You'll have to ask Dylan."

"Continue," he said.

As best she could, she explained what had happened when they got to the kayak shack. She probably shouldn't have left the vehicle. But if she hadn't, Tank might not have made it.

"That's when Dylan should have called," he said. "I should have been part of that bust at the kayak shack."

"Dylan didn't want it to be a bust and neither did I. Tank was helping us voluntarily. It doesn't seem right for him to be arrested for that."

"He won't be," Woody said. "He'll be arrested for hacking into an NSA database last month."

"If he survives," she said darkly. While she had been apologizing to the Buena Vista staff, she'd gotten an update on Tank's condition. After his surgery, which had gone well, Tank was in an induced coma. Tomorrow, they would wake him.

"He'll be fine."

"I'm hiring an attorney for him," she said. "You can't ask questions until the attorney is in place."

"You haven't been a whole lot of help, Doctor."

"Nor have you," she said. "May I ask a question?"

"Go ahead."

"If I operate on Diego Romero and make it possible for him to regain his memory, am I breaking any laws?"

"Why the hell would you want to do that?"

"I'm a doctor," she said. "It's my job to cure my patients, not to judge them. If Koslov had come to me and asked for my assistance, I might have gone along with his plan."

The door to Grace McHenry's office crashed open. Dylan stood facing them. His tone was serious. "You can't operate. Don't even think about it."

"Why not?"

"Diego Romero isn't like anyone you've ever met. He doesn't operate by the same standards of right and wrong. Don't make me run through the whole litany of terrible things he's done. Help me, Woody."

"What are you doing in here?" Woody stood behind the desk. "Were you eavesdropping?"

Dylan removed his earbud. "Jayne has one of these. It transmits both ways."

Jayne touched her ear. "My receiver is turned off. I couldn't hear him, but he heard me."

"Obviously."

She stood and faced Dylan. "You see the differences in Diego Romero. I see the similarities. His heart pumps the same way yours does…or mine. His brain is constructed the same way."

"If he were dead, the world would be a better place."

"That's not your call," she said. "As a doctor, I don't get to decide who lives and who dies. It's my job to patch people up and send them on their way."

Dylan came toward her. Totally disregarding Agent

Woody, he embraced her. "I agree with you in theory, Jayne. I really do, but I don't want anything bad to happen to you. Romero doesn't leave witnesses. He'll kill you."

"Not if I save his life," she said.

"He won't care. As soon as you're done with him, you're a dead woman."

The smooth, handsome Javier Flores rushed through the door. Her dad was right behind him.

Javier said, "We must go. Koslov has been sighted at the hospital."

Her father grasped her wrist, attempting to literally drag her away from Dylan. "Seriously," he growled, "we're all in danger."

"Stop it." Woody waved his arms. "Everyone settle down."

Then she heard the echo of gunfire from down the hall.

Dylan couldn't tell where the shots were coming from. There was a lot of firepower at the Buena Vista hospital, including Sheriff Swanson and his deputies and the federal agents and his brother, Sean. Their presence didn't seem to deter the assault from Koslov and his men.

He would have liked to grab Jayne's hand and run for cover, but they encountered resistance at every turn. The sheriff's men directed them toward a supposedly safe exit. Her father clung to her. The two of them had a lot to clean up, but that conversation was more suited to a psychotherapist's office than a gun battle in a hospital.

Through his earbud, Dylan heard his brother's voice. "Don't come to the ER entrance. Koslov and his men are coming in through these doors."

Their "supposedly safe exit" had been compromised. He separated Jayne from the others and guided her into the OR and recovery unit, which was now deserted. For the moment, they were alone.

"There's something I need to tell you," he said.

He didn't lift his gaze, didn't look into her eyes, and he realized that he was scared about how she'd respond. Ironic! They faced real-life bullets, the kind that can kill, and he was afraid of what she'd say to him, how she could hurt him.

"What is it, Dylan?"

"I quit."

She stopped dead in her tracks. "You picked a real bad time to tell me you're not going to be my body-guard."

"Not what I meant." He pivoted to face her. "I quit because I don't want to work for you. We need to be equals...as much as we can be."

"I haven't been treating you like an employee," she huffed. "I don't sleep with my employees."

"Not what I meant...again."

The pop-pop-pop of gunfire became clearer. It seemed like the shooters were just outside the recovery unit. And they were looking for her. Jayne was the object of their search.

He had to get her to safety. Adrenaline flooded his

brain and gave him clarity. He grasped her hand and gave a light tug. As they went forward, he spoke in a calm voice.

"Equals," he said, "in terms of what we both bring to the table. We both have money. We're both successful. The sex is good."

"Yes, the sex is very good."

He admitted, "I'm fairly sure that you're smarter than I am, but that can't be helped."

Determining their route purely by instinct, he went left at one corner, then right at the next. Much of their time together had been spent chasing through corridors and staircases. He was beginning to feel like a rat in a maze or one of those cartoon characters in early video games that hopped from one area to another. He'd spent hours playing those games. Given all that time, he ought to be better at this.

She stopped to catch her breath and looked up at him. "I can't believe we're having a relationship discussion right now."

"This might be the perfect time." Most guys, like him, believed that gunfire made appropriate background noise for a talk about their relationship.

"Well, you're right. You and I are very well matched."

"Live with me, Jayne. At my house in Denver."

"Until the danger is over?"

"I was thinking of something more permanent."

It was too soon to make this kind of commitment. But in a flash of adrenaline-fueled intelligence, he saw himself standing beside her with two small children—their children—playing in the yard. They were such a perfect fit.

"We agree on one thing," she said. "I don't want you to be my bodyguard." She twisted her head, looking toward the door. "I want you out of the bodyguard business, entirely."

"What? Why?"

She gestured angrily in the direction of the gunfire. "Danger, I don't want you to be in danger."

"What about my brother? What about Mason? I can't just leave TST Security in the lurch."

"They're big boys. They can take care of themselves. You don't need this job. You've already made a fortune with your computer games and designs. That's where your real interest lies."

She had a point, but there was no way he'd abandon his brother and his best friend. He could work something out, figure a way around her demand. *A demand?* Where did she get off making demands on him?

A loud burst of gunfire outside the door alerted him. They needed to change position. Exiting through the other door into this area, they charged down a narrow corridor that ended at a door. Other doors along the way were closed.

He jiggled the handle; it was locked. The sign outside the door indicated that this was an entrance to the pharmacy. Dylan picked the lock and they slipped into the darkened room, carefully walking past shelves stocked with all manner of bottles and containers. The front wall of the pharmacy was reinforced windows from the waist to ceiling with the blinds drawn. At the far left was a windowed door with a wide counter for picking up prescriptions.

He peered over the edge of the counter and lifted the blind so he could see. He was looking into the main entrance lobby and waiting area.

They ducked beneath the counter. In the shadows, he could see only a faint outline of her face and her long hair. He pushed his glasses up on his nose. "Will you move in with me, Jayne?"

"I have a house, and I'm only halfway through renovations."

"You'll like my place. I have a home gym, a couple of offices, outdoor barbecue…" He stopped himself before he got into square footage and number of bathrooms. He sounded like a real estate agent. "This isn't about where we live. Only that we're together."

Her fingers clenched around his. "Are you asking me to marry you?"

He'd been trying to avoid using that specific term. "Not really… This is more about living together."

"Oh, Dylan, I don't know. I can't say."

"If you want to be together, we can work out the details."

"Details first," she said. "I won't let you railroad me. I still have a lot I want to do in my career."

"I won't stop you. I'm proud of you."

He heard a disturbance in the area outside the pharmacy window. Peeking over the ledge, he saw several people dressed in scrubs racing across the lobby. Evacuation was under way.

Moments later, he saw two men in camouflage fatigues. Their boots pounded on the smooth vinyl flooring. They were jogging in formation. How many were there? Had Koslov recruited an army?

Through his earbud, he communicated with Sean. "We need an exit strategy."

His brother replied immediately, "I got separated from the vehicle. I suggest you try to get a ride with somebody else."

"Got it," Dylan said.

She gave him a puzzled look. "What?"

"I was talking to my brother on the earbud."

She reached for her own ear. "I don't know how you keep those things straight with me in one ear and your brother in the other."

When she started to remove her earbud, he stopped her. "Keep it in. Might come in handy to be able to hear you when you're three hundred yards away."

"Why? I have it turned off."

"But I can still hear you, and I like being inside your ear." He cupped her chin, leaned forward and kissed her. After all they'd been through tonight, she still smelled good, and her lips were as soft as rose petals.

He separated from her and sat with his back against the door under the counter. "My timing sucks."

"Yeah, it kind of does."

He frowned. "By the by, there's no way in hell I'd quit my job just because you tell me to."

"And I refuse to leave my house until I'm ready." A tiny smile lifted the corner of her mouth. "It's always going to be like this between us. We've both got busy lives, full lives with very little extra time."

He heard someone approaching and peeked over the window ledge. "It's your dad and Javier. I'm going to call them over."

"Why?" She groaned. "I don't want to go with them."

"Sean can't get to our SUV. Your dad might be your best way out of here."

"Let me stay with you."

"Too dangerous." He stood, pulled up the blinds that had been covering the window and rapped on the glass. When he had Javier's attention, he got the lock on the door unfastened.

Javier caught hold of Jayne's upper arm. "Come with us. We have a vehicle."

That was all Dylan needed to hear. He stepped back into the shadows and watched as she was pulled away from him.

She turned back toward him. "I'll talk to you later."

"Count on it."

Chapter Twenty-One

Held between her father and Javier Flores, Jayne ran for the exit. She wished that Dylan was here. Without him, she felt unprotected. Had Javier checked to make sure none of Koslov's army were waiting for them in the lobby? Was he armed? She knew her dad had a pistol in his pocket. Years ago, he'd gotten a "concealed carry" permit.

They ran down a short sidewalk and jumped into a vehicle. Javi and her father got in back. She was in the passenger seat. The driver had his jacket collar turned up and wore his baseball cap low on his forehead.

Not much of a disguise. She recognized him. "Koslov."

Panic flared behind her eyelids. Her nervous systems went on high alert. Her brain told her to leap from the moving vehicle and run to safety. But she was paralyzed, every muscle clenched.

She turned and looked into the backseat. Her father had passed out and slumped unconscious against the door. Javier Flores had a gun aimed in her direction.

"What did you do to him?"

"I administered an injection to make him sleep," Javi said. "I have no intention of harming your father though he has profited greatly from dealings with my family. It's just business. I've taken my share from him."

She'd thought it was odd for him to be tagging along throughout their cat-and-mouse game, running here and running there. A bulwark of anger rose up and blocked her fear and the panicky feelings of helplessness. Javier Flores had betrayed her father and led him into the hands of his enemies. "What are you after?"

"I want you to perform your miracle surgery and bring back the memory of Diego Romero."

"Why?"

"Somewhere in those lost memories are people and places and numbers for bank accounts that are important to certain members of my family."

If she hadn't been so furious, she would have laughed. Among the details the old man had forgotten were the pieces needed to access the ill-gotten gains of Javier's family...locations of safe-deposit boxes, account numbers, portfolio information. It would serve Javier right if the old man never recalled that particular data.

Turning in the seat, she stared through the windshield. She knew who was really in charge here—the man driving the car. "You finally have me, Koslov. What do you want me to do?"

"I don't want to hurt you," he said in his oddly accented voice. "I could have killed you and your boyfriend several times, but I didn't. I could have killed the hacker, Sherman. But that didn't happen. All I ask of you is to heal my father."

"Diego Romero is your father?"

"Yes, and my mother was Elena Petrovski, an exotic Russian beauty. I am named Koslov after an uncle."

A strange way to talk about his mother, but she guessed Koslov had a lot of psychotic, weird problems when it came to family and relationships. "Your accent," she said. "Is it partly Russian?"

"My mother's influence. Her photograph, taken in the nightclub where she worked, still makes my father smile. After his stroke, he lost memory of almost everything else. I want you to operate on him."

"You asked me this before," she said, half-remembering their conversation in the parking structure.

"And you agreed to operate. You said that you are a doctor, and doctors are obligated to help whenever they can. You will cure him."

She wasn't sure what would happen, but she was afraid that Dylan had called it correctly when he'd said that Koslov would kill her—and now her father, too—when he no longer had a use for her.

"I'll do my best," she said.

A⊤ ᴛᴇɴ ᴍɪɴᴜᴛᴇs past three o'clock in the morning, the conference room in the Buena Vista sheriff's office was filled with law-enforcement personnel: cops, feds and deputies. Dylan had taken a position near a table at the rear exit where a forty-two-cup stainless-steel coffee-maker belched steam and squirted a dark, slightly filmy liquid into disposable cups. He stared toward the front of the room, where Jayne's father leaned his elbows on a podium.

Peter the Great looked like hell. He'd aged twenty years in twenty minutes. The collar on his shirt was open. His necktie hung loose. His suit was rumpled, and his perfectly trimmed hair stood out in messy clumps. His eyes looked like he hadn't slept in weeks. According to Sheriff Swanson, Peter had stumbled onto a porch at the north end of town and hammered at the door until the family inside responded. They called the police and a patrol car picked him up.

Swanson introduced him and asked for questions.

One of the officers called out, "You were in the vehicle with Koslov. Did he say where he was going?"

"I was drugged," Shackleford said wearily. "I don't remember much."

"Who is Javier Flores?"

"I thought he was my friend. I knew him and his family because we're all involved in the Venezuelan oil business." His mouth tensed as he fought back tears. "I'm not a hundred percent sure, but I think Javi gave me an injection in the thigh. Everything went blank."

Sheriff Swanson added, "We are operating under the theory that Javier Flores is working with Koslov."

"They have my daughter." Shackleford's voice cracked.

"The only thing I can tell you that might be useful is that she agreed to do neurosurgery on Diego Romero. The operation takes five hours. That's all the time we have to find her."

"Unless Koslov has already taken her out of town," the sheriff said as he took the podium and gestured for Peter to sit. "The airports, including private facilities for small planes, were immediately shut down."

Dylan hoped they'd acted in time. If Jayne was in the air, on her way to Caracas, there wasn't much he could do to find her. The sheriff and his men had verified that the local hospitals and clinics were not being used for the surgery on Romero. Highway surveillance cameras had been activated.

In three hours, it would be dawn. That was when Agent Woody and the feds could start helicopter sweeps of the area. Dylan figured the overhead surveillance would be their best chance. Koslov must have set up a clinic in a house or cabin. But how would he know that they'd be in this area? Koslov didn't know about RSQ Ranch. Why would he establish his operating theater nearby?

Sean nudged his shoulder. "Let's get out of here before somebody gives us a time-wasting assignment."

"The way I figure," Dylan said, "Koslov assembled the operating room in a motorhome or in the rear of a semitrailer. That way, he wasn't tied to a location."

"You need coffee," his brother said. "Real coffee, not this swill."

"I need Jayne. How could I have let her go?"

"You got played, little brother. It happens. Even to geniuses like you and Jayne. That Javier guy probably had Jayne's dad running all over the hospital, looking for her. When they found her, you did what you thought was best."

Dylan hated being wrong. He went into an adjoining room to check on the network of computer surveillance that was searching for any sign of Jayne, such as using a credit card or a phone. A deputy and a fed were assigned to that job. Both were competent. They weren't Tank, but they'd do okay.

Sean gave him a shove. "We're going. Now."

"But what if…"

"Leave this end of the search to the sheriff and Woody. They're bureaucrats. They know how to do this stuff."

"You're right." Pacing up and down these corridors was making him crazy.

IN THE CAR, Sean drove. He headed back toward Denver, which was the opposite direction of most of the other searchers. The night began to thin. Stars faded, and the half-moon disappeared.

"When you interrogated that guy," Dylan said, "how could you be sure he was telling the truth?"

Woody had taken advantage of Sean's FBI training in profiling and questioning suspects. He used Sean to interview one of Koslov's men who had been injured and hadn't escaped with the others.

Without bragging, Sean said, "I'm pretty good at interrogation. And I only had one thing I needed to find out—if they were going to take Jayne on a plane."

"How did you get him to talk?"

"He's a paid mercenary and doesn't have any grand ideals he's hanging on to. I didn't hurt him. Torture isn't my style. But I didn't give him the pain meds, either. And I might have hinted about how he was going to lose his leg if I didn't let the doctor see him."

"Sounds like the way you'd question me when we were kids."

"Natural talent," his brother said. "Anyway, this guy babbled and doubled back and made a lot of mistakes. Taking her away on an airplane wasn't part of the plan. I guarantee that the old man—Diego Romero himself—is here in Colorado."

"Waiting for Jayne."

The search for a decent cup of coffee led them to one of the more expensive lodges in town. Sean drove down a winding road, then another, then another. He tried to find areas with wide overlooks where they could stop and scan the valley.

The sun was up, and the minutes were ticking down. Dylan figured they only had an hour and a half before she'd be done with the surgery.

Sean asked, "Are you in love with her?"

"I'm afraid so." He scanned the landscape outside

the windows, using the binoculars when something looked promising. "I asked her to move in with me. She said no."

"Are you going to let that stop you?"

"Hell, no."

He would get her back. He had to bring her back to him. And he would never let her go. They rounded another curve and… Dylan heard a crackle in his ear. The bud was coming to life. He glanced at Sean. "Did you hear that?"

"Jayne must have figured out how to turn it on."

"I think it's been on all the time. We were too far away to pick up the signal. Transmissions in the mountains are tricky."

But the bud was transmitting now.

Chapter Twenty-Two

The thread of sound connecting them gave Dylan fresh hope. He hadn't given up on finding them, but the odds had been stacked against them. He'd never let her go again. Whatever it took, they would be together.

He heard Jayne clearly as she said, "I'll close his skull. In about an hour, I should know if the operation was a success."

The next voice was that of Javier Flores. "Can he talk now? Can he answer questions?"

Jane spoke up. "I have to ask you to step away from the enclosed area. Your clothes aren't sanitized."

A weak voice spoke a stream of Spanish that Dylan knew was peppered with profanity. He murmured, "That must be the old man."

"One question," Javier said, "just one question. I need to know the name of the bank with the safe-deposit box. That's where this old dog stashed the codes to accounts filled with my family's money."

That explained why Javier was so involved in retrieving Romero's memories.

He heard Jayne speaking in Spanish, asking Romero if he had anything he wanted to say to Javier. There was a mumble, then Jayne translated. "He says you should go to the devil."

He wished that she could give them a clue as to where she was. He heard the beeping and buzzing of the many machines in the background and remembered her doing this surgery in Denver.

Another voice intruded, "Get away from my father, Flores."

It was Koslov.

Sean drove to the left at a fork in the road. "Talk to her, Dylan. Maybe she can hear you."

That obvious thought hadn't even occurred to him. He'd been so thrilled to hear her voice that his brain had disconnected. "Jayne," he whispered, "it's Dylan. If you can hear me, say morning."

Her response was immediate. "Wonder what the weather will be like this morning?"

He asked, "Where are you?"

"You know, Koslov, I still can't help but marvel at what you've done here. You turned this ugly white motor home into a traveling neurosurgery center. Will you leave it here for me? I could help so many people with this."

"When will you be finished?" Koslov asked.

"Like I said, in about an hour I'll be able to tell if the operation was a success."

There were rustling noises, and he imagined her taking off her sterile gown and gloves.

Sean pulled onto the gravelly shoulder of the two-lane mountain road. Their SUV was at a high point. Sean took the binoculars, climbed out of the car and scanned the rocky ridges and thick forests below. He pointed. "Can you see it? A white-and-gold motor home with the sun glaring off the side?"

"Jayne," Dylan said, "we're going to get you out of there. Be ready. I'm signing off for a few minutes, but don't worry. I'll be back."

He adjusted his earbud so he could hear her but she couldn't hear him, and he motioned for his brother to do the same. For a long moment, they stood side by side in front of the SUV, squinting into the rising sun at the faraway reflection off the motor home where Jayne was being held.

"We found her," Sean said.

"Damn right, we did."

Dylan let go with a wild cheer, Sean did the same, and they threw their arms around each other. Everything was going to be all right.

Sean broke contact. "Koslov had an army when he came through the hospital. We need to find them, and arrange for backup."

"There's only one thing I'm worried about," Dylan said. "How do I get Jayne out of that tin can? As long as she's trapped in there with Koslov, Javi and the old man, she's in danger."

"You'll figure it out," his brother said. "It's a matter of mechanics, plays right into your talents."

He was right. Dylan had been training all his life for a moment like this when he had to figure out how to steal the princess from the trolls in their fortress.

He remembered all the machines in Jayne's operating theater. Likewise, the motor home OR needed a power source, a generator and something to regulate the temperature and humidity. That plain-looking motor home had been customized. There had to be a way for Dylan to break in and rescue Jayne.

Rushing back to the car, he issued instructions. "Take me as close to the motor home as you can without being seen. Then you go back and coordinate everything with the backup."

"What are you going to do?"

"Protect Jayne."

THE INTERIOR OF the motor home was surprisingly spacious. There was room for Jayne and all of her neurosurgery equipment at the rear. In the center section, there was a bed where Romero was resting and recovering. A small table and chairs were arranged near the steering wheel. The windows were completely blanked out. No one could see in or out. If she'd been afflicted with claustrophobia, she never would have been able to function in this space.

But she'd performed well, better than she'd expected. In the usual course of a long operation like this, she took breaks when other docs and specialists were check-ing and referencing MRIs and other material. Today's surgery was nonstop except for one pause when she'd insisted on stretching and hydrating. She would have liked a walk, but Koslov wouldn't let her leave the motor home; she feared she would never see daylight again.

Sitting at the table with Javi opposite her and Ko-slov behind him, she tried to lift her teacup. No use. Her fingers were trembling too much.

"Something wrong?" Javi asked. He turned his arm so he could see the face of his gold wristwatch. "We have thirty-nine minutes to go."

Not if Dylan could rescue her first. "Then what?" she asked. "If the operation is a success, what happens to me?"

"I can't exactly set you free," Javi said. "I might be able to talk my way out of the situation, claiming I was captured by Koslov and Romero. You are, unfortunately, an eye witness."

"I won't say anything," she said. "I promise."

"There's no need to beg for your life," he said with a sneer. "My decision is already made."

Koslov cleared his throat. "I make the decisions. Not you."

A slight twitch at the corner of Javi's eye betrayed his fear of the assassin. Koslov was the alpha wolf; he didn't need to say much or make threats. Danger oozed from him. If she hoped for any sort of concession, he was the one she ought to negotiate with.

"I saved your father," she said. "That must count for something."

Javi corrected her. "His life wasn't in danger."

"But his memory was lost," she said. "My surgery helped him. What do you think, Koslov?"

"You're a strange woman."

"Maybe you could donate all this equipment to me and my hospital," she suggested. "Or arrange for me to travel to Venezuela to consult with neurosurgeons there."

Javi held up his fancy gold watch. "Twenty-two minutes left."

Hurry, Dylan, hurry. She didn't know how long she could stall. She assumed that he and Sean had gone to get backup. Koslov had several other men, but she didn't know where they were. They could be surrounding the motor home or could be sleeping. In the meantime, her life was measured by the tick-tick-tick of the second hand on Javi's fancy watch.

"I could be your father's nurse," she offered.

"You're overqualified."

Great! She'd finally found a man who appreciated her skills, and he was getting ready to kill her. "I'll do whatever you want."

Koslov rose and walked toward her. When he placed his hand on her shoulder, she fought the urge to flinch. He leaned close to her ear. In his strangely accented voice, he said, "I promise you a fast death. You won't feel a thing."

All the fear she'd been holding in check gushed through her. Her heart shattered. Her bones melted. If she hadn't heard a crackle in her ear, she would have come completely undone.

Abruptly, she stood. Jayne didn't want to take a chance on having Koslov hear a sound from the earbud.

"Jayne." Dylan's voice was a whisper. "Go to the back of the motor home. As far back as you can go on the driver's side."

She snapped her fingers as though remembering a detail. "There are a few readouts I need to check. Then I'll do the final tests on your father."

"I'm impressed," Javi said, "with how professional you are. You're showing no fear."

"Maybe I can't believe you're going to hurt me after I did such a good job," she said. "Maybe I think there's still something good and ethical in you."

"Really?"

Not at all, not a bit. She truly believed that these three men were evil. Dylan had warned her from the start. "Maybe."

As she passed through the middle section, Diego Romero gave her a weak smile. Koslov followed her. He eyed her suspiciously.

When she reached the back of the motor home, she picked up a readout of neuromuscular activity and followed the center line with her finger. "Here I am," she said so Dylan would know. "Back in the corner with my readouts."

Koslov stopped at the edge of the back section. "What are you doing?"

"I wanted to make a quick check on the interface between the neural olfactory and the limbic systems." She tossed out a few more terms that she hoped he didn't understand.

In her ear, Dylan said, "When I tell you, I want you to duck down."

Javi stepped up behind Koslov, watching and listening. He glanced down at the old man in the bed. In Spanish, he asked the location of the safe-deposit box for the funds of the Flores family.

Without hesitation, Romero said, *"Banco Federal Caracas."*

Javi laughed as he took his gun from the side holster under his jacket. "I'm done. Don't have to stick around."

Quick as a rattlesnake, Koslov whipped out his Glock and fired one bullet into the center of Javi's forehead. A mist of blood and matter surrounded Javi's skull before his legs crumpled.

"Duck!"

The lights in the motor home went out.

Darkness covered her. Jayne sank into a crouch.

Before she had a chance to react, she felt Dylan's hands on her arms. Though she couldn't see, she knew it was him. She recognized his touch and his scent as he dragged her backward. The machine that had been against the wall was gone and they were sliding into a luggage compartment, packed tightly with a generator and air-conditioning equipment.

When the lights in her house had been cut, she'd been terrified. This was different. This time, she blessed the darkness that would help her escape.

When Dylan flipped open the door to the compartment, the morning sunlight blinded her. She staggered to her feet.

He grasped her hand. "Run."

As they dashed through the tall grasses toward the forest, she heard gunfire. She saw Koslov's men taking aim and firing at the sheriff, the deputies, the police and others. And she imagined bullets whizzing past them, barely missing. When she and Dylan hit the forest, he pulled her into the shelter of the trees and embraced her.

"You're safe now," he said. "I've got you."

Though not aware of crying, her cheeks were damp. And she was tired, so tired that she felt limp. "I can't stand up, can't stand."

"No problem." He lowered them to the ground, leaned his back against a rock and held her.

"This feels like heaven," she said. "How did you figure out how to get me?"

"I'm the guy," he said. "I can fix any security system and that goes double for motor homes rigged to generators."

"That's right. When we first met, you promised a repair job at my house."

"If you're still planning to live there."

She gazed into his warm gray eyes. "My house or yours. Wherever we stay, I want to be together."

"Living together," he said.

"Isn't that what people do when they're in love?"

"I love you, Jayne."

A few moments ago, she'd expected to be dead. And now…he loved her. And she felt the same way about him. She snuggled closer in his arms, aware that the battle had gone quiet.

She exhaled a sigh. "I guess we should report in and let people know we're okay."

He helped her stand and offered his arm for her to lean on. She gestured him away, not wanting to show that she couldn't support herself.

Dylan's brother came toward them. After he gave her a hug, he reported, "Only a few injuries on our side. Koslov and his men are in custody, several are injured. Javier Flores is dead."

"What about Romero?" she asked.

"He's in good shape, and he's a regular chatterbox. The FBI is all over him."

She recognized a voice and turned toward it. "Dad?"

He held his arms open. "I have a lot to apologize for."

"Yes." Damn right he had a lot to be sorry for, starting with firing Dylan and ending with turning her over to Koslov. She wrapped her arms around him. It was better not to dwell in the past. "Let's start fresh."

"You've got it, sweetheart."

She looked her father in the eye. "Dylan and I are moving in together."

Peter the Great swallowed hard. "Do you love him?"

"So very, very much."

"You've got my blessing."

She slipped back into Dylan's waiting arms. This was all the shelter she would ever need.

* * * * *

INTRIGUE

Available December 20, 2016

SPECIAL EXCERPT FROM

MIRA®

A popular girl goes missing, and everyone close to her has something to hide.

*Go inside the mind of a criminal in the fourth book in the riveting **THE PROFILER** series: STALKED by Elizabeth Heiter.*

"Where are you, Haley?" Linda whispered into the stillness of her daughter's room.

Today marked exactly a month since her daughter had gone missing. Since Haley's boyfriend, Jordan, had dropped her off at school for cheerleading practice. Since her best friend Marissa had waved to her from the field on that unusually warm day, watched her walk into the school, presumably to change before joining Marissa at practice.

She'd never walked out again.

How did a teenage girl go missing from *inside* her high school? No one could answer that for Linda. As time went by, they seemed to have fewer answers and more questions.

But Linda *knew*—with some deep part of her she could only explain as mother's intuition—that Haley was out there somewhere. Not buried in an unmarked grave, as she'd overheard two cops speculating when day after day passed with no more clues. Haley was still alive, and just waiting for someone to bring her home.

Linda clutched Haley's bright pink sweatshirt tighter. She fell against the bed, trying to hold her sobs in, and the mattress slid away from her, away from the box spring.

Linda froze as the edge of a tiny black notebook caught her attention.

The book was jammed between the box spring and the bed frame. The police must have missed it, because she'd seen them peer underneath Haley's mattress when they'd looked through the room, assessing her daughter's things so matter-of-factly.

Linda's pulse skyrocketed as she yanked it out. She didn't recognize the notebook, but when she opened the cover, there was no mistaking her daughter's girlie handwriting. And the words…

She dropped the notebook, practically flung it away from her in her desire to get rid of it, to unsee it. She didn't realize she'd started screaming until her husband ran into the room and wrapped his arms around her.

"What? What is it?" he kept asking, but all she could do was sob and point a shaking hand at the notebook, lying open to the first page, and Haley's distinctive scrawl:

If you're reading this, I'm already dead.

Follow FBI profiler Evelyn Baine as she tries to uncover which of Haley's secrets might have led to her disappearance.

STALKED
by Elizabeth Heiter
Available December 27, 2016,
from MIRA Books.

$1.00 OFF

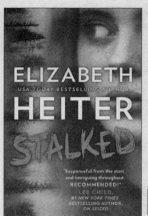

$7.99 U.S./$9.99 CAN.

ELIZABETH HEITER

Secrets can be deadly...

STALKED

MIRA®

Available December 27, 2016

Order your copy today!

- ✂

$1.00 OFF

the purchase price of STALKED by Elizabeth Heiter.

Offer valid from December 17, 2016, to June 17, 2017.
Redeemable at participating retail outlets, in-store only. Not redeemable at Barnes & Noble. Limit one coupon per purchase. Valid in the U.S.A. and Canada only.

® and ™ are trademarks owned and used by the trademark owner and/or its licensee.

© 2016 Harlequin Enterprises Limited

MCOUPEH1216